SHADOWS IN THE JUNGLE

A Paul Phillips Mystery

Philip DeLizio

Dr. Philip DeLizio, Ed. D. is a retired school teacher.

<u>Books</u>

<u>Young Adult Inspirational</u>

Rekindled Faith

A Light on the Horizon

From Darkness to Light

Emma's Dilemma

A Letter of Hope

Crossroads

<u>Paul Phillips Mysteries</u>

Twisted Reckonings

Shadows in the Jungle

The Missing Piece

The Cricketers Conspiracy

Shadows of the Past

Dedication

For my son Anthony

PREFACE

In the serene paradise of St. Anne, retired detective Paul Phillips is drawn into a gripping mystery when a fellow islander goes missing. As he delves into the case, Paul uncovers secrets that powerful people will kill to keep hidden. With his determination to seek the truth, Paul finds himself in the crosshairs of dangerous enemies who want the case closed permanently. Navigating through false leads and tight-lipped locals, Paul relies on his experience and keen observation to separate facts from fiction. His pursuit leads to wider corruption on the island, and with lives at stake, Paul casts away his retired life for one last stand against the evil that plagues the island. It will take all his cunning and courage to prevent more blood from being spilled and serve the justice this serene paradise so desperately needs. "Shadows in the Jungle" is a gripping mystery/crime thriller that weaves together intrigue, danger, and the pursuit of justice in a small tropical community.

CONTENTS

CHAPTER ONE

A Quiet Life Disturbed

PAUL TOOK A DEEP BREATH OF THE SALTY SEA AIR, SAVORING THE fleeting peace of the new day. He's a retired detective who has seen it all. His years on the force have left him with a cynical outlook on life but also a deep-seated sense of justice and duty.

Before finding peace and comfort on St. Anne, he spent his days in a bustling U.S. city, working as a detective with a large metropolitan police force. To this day, he refuses to name the city. The concrete jungle was a far cry from the serene shores he now calls home. But even amid the chaos, his sense of justice never wavered. Now, the island's calm exterior hides a storm of secrets waiting to be uncovered.

Paul found little satisfaction in avoiding what stirred his soul. As he straightened books on the old and crooked bookcase, a well-worn volume fell open to faded notes scribbled during his early cases. His success had come from honing his gifts, not suppressing them. Retirement was meant to provide leisure, yet an unquiet mind found no peace.

He is a man of few words, preferring to observe and gather information before forming opinions. He is patient and methodical, traits that served him well in his former career. However, he can also be gruff and impatient when dealing with those he perceives as incompetent or untrustworthy.

Despite his tough exterior, Paul cares deeply about the people around him, especially those who have suffered at the hands of criminals. He is not one to seek recognition or praise for his actions but rather finds satisfaction in knowing that he's made a difference. As a retired detective living on the Caribbean Island of St. Anne, Paul enjoys spending his days relaxing on the beach, sipping rum, and fishing.

He has been living peacefully these past few months, more peacefully since he solved the one case he thought unsolvable, the one case that haunted him for years, the one case that nearly cost the life of a fine police officer, Zoe Walker.

St. Anne has been Paul's home for the past six years, a Caribbean gem that holds a special place in Paul's heart. This island is a vivid tapestry of natural beauty and fascinating history. For Paul, what makes it truly captivating is its rich French-infused heritage. St. Anne is blessed with stunning landscapes that seem straight out of a postcard. From the pristine white sand beaches, gently lapped by the azure waters of the Caribbean Sea, to the lush rainforests teeming with exotic flora and wildlife, it is a paradise for the senses. But what really sets St. Anne apart is its history, steeped in French influence. The island was once a French colony, and remnants of that heritage are visible everywhere. The charming architecture, the quaint fishing villages, and the delicious culinary delights all bear the mark of French culture.

One cannot help but fall in love with the island's unique blend of Caribbean charm and French sophistication. The friendly locals, known for their warm hospitality, add to the allure of this remarkable place. Whether it is exploring the vibrant local markets, indulging in authentic French-Caribbean cuisine, or simply strolling along the waterfront, there is always something new to discover.

For Paul, St. Anne is not just a beautiful island; it is a refuge. It allows him to escape the shadows of his past and immerse himself in the tranquility of its surroundings. The soothing sound of the waves and the breathtaking sunsets serve as a constant reminder that there is still beauty and peace to be found in this troubled world. It is a place where he can find solace, and perhaps even redemption.

Mornings were Paul's favorite time of day. Sunrise brings a burst of fiery hues, painting the sky in vibrant oranges and pinks, a fleeting moment of tranquility before the day's challenges unfold. Although, he is fond of sunsets as well when the horizon is ablaze with molten gold, a stark contrast to the darkness that prowls the island's underbelly.

The beach, with its soft sands and seagulls' cries, is a beacon of solace where troubles temporarily recede. But beneath the surface lies a world of secrets and unspoken truths, waiting to be unraveled.

Most people would describe Paul as cynical; Paul prefers to call himself a healthy skeptic, a questioning of the facade that masks the darker truths in this world. In Paul's previous line of work, there was little room for naivety. One must peel back the layers to see the raw core of things.

A flash of movement drew his gaze to the back of his bungalow, where his driveway ended at his back door. His brow furrowed at the sight of Officer Mackenzie of the St. Anne Police Department showing up at his home alone. Something was amiss for her to come herself on her day off. As she strode up to Paul, her grim expression confirmed his suspicion.

"We've had another disappearance, this time in the north village." She shared the barest details: "A woman named Jane Munro, last seen two nights ago, has disappeared. All that is known about her at this point is she used to work at the local bookstore."

The Seashell Pages is a charming little bookstore located in the center of town, owned since it first opened 25 years ago by Mrs. Jenkins, a kind lady with a passion for literature. Paul listened attentively, piecing together implications beneath her concise report. Too many pieces didn't add up, from Jane's purported activities to the timeline of the search thus far.

As she approached Paul, he noticed her sharp gaze and no-nonsense demeanor. Mackenzie is in her mid-30s, with auburn hair, which was pulled back in a practical ponytail and clear green eyes that miss nothing. Since this was supposed to be her day off, she was dressed casually yet professionally in a fitted t-shirt, jeans, and sturdy boots, a hint of her dedication to the job even outside duty hours. Her general attitude exudes a mix of skepticism and curiosity, as if she's constantly assessing the situation while secretly intrigued by the mystery at hand.

Officer Mackenzie has about a decade of experience in law enforcement under her belt. She's seen her fair share of cases and knows the ins and outs of police work on the island. Despite her relative youth in the force, most of the cops have nearly 20 years under their belts, Mackenzie's sharp instincts and dedication make her a valuable asset in navigating the complexities of any case.

She began to explain why she was working on her day off. The disappearance of Jane Munro had stirred up something unsettling in her. Her commitment to serving justice and her suspicions about the case pushed her to delve into the investigation even outside her regular hours.

"Hey, Paul. Sorry to intrude on your retirement, but I couldn't shake off this nagging feeling. The case of Jane Munro's disappearance has been keeping me up at night. I needed to discuss some things with you, off the record. Hope you don't mind me showing up unannounced."

It seems the mystery at hand resonated with Mackenzie's sense of duty, prompting her to go the extra mile to uncover the truth behind Jane's disappearance.

Paul agreed to accompany her to the crime scene but made no guarantees he would help. "Alright, Mackenzie, I'll accompany you to the crime scene. Can't promise I'll get involved, but I'll take a look. No guarantees beyond that."

Mackenzie nodded, "I appreciate your willingness to at least check it out, Paul. Your insights could be invaluable, even if it's just a quick glance. Let's head there together."

She seemed relieved yet determined, understanding my cautious stance but hoping for more.

Paul's reluctance to help was not because he didn't want to help, rather he was still recovering from the near loss of the last detective from the St. Anne Police Department who asked for his help: Zoe Walker.

Zoe was nearly killed by a crazed murderer as Paul and Zoe were trying to solve a tough homicide case. After the case was solved, Zoe accepted a position with the police department on the neighboring island of Guadeloupe. Paul still feels responsible for the near tragedy.

With his morning routine now complete, or rather interrupted, Paul was on his way with Officer Mackenzie to the location of the disappearance of Jane Munro, keen eyes and experience primed to find what local law enforcement had overlooked. With a steady gait, he walked, leaving behind the pretense of an easy life for one truer to his nature and to justice this community deserved.

Following Mackenzie back to her car, Paul's retirement slipped further from his mind. His gift for observation noted every contradictory aspect of the "crime scene," from erased clues in the sand to half-hearted questioning of villagers. While others saw tragedy, Paul saw opportunity, a chance for justice perhaps long denied these people.

As they drove into town, the day's serenity faded under a shadow of unease. Paul's senses tingled with a stirring beneath the surface, and his curiosity piqued to know what mysteries the jungle now concealed.

Thinking back to just before Officer Mackenzie arrived, Paul was content with drinking his coffee, tending to the morning chores that filled his days, watering tropical plants that gave his home its inviting aroma, and walking along the beach thinking of better days ahead. For most, such simplicities offered fulfillment after careers chasing darkness.

The drive from Paul's tranquil abode to the crime scene with Mackenzie was not what he would consider a leisurely Sunday cruise. The engine's hum was a backdrop to the tense silence that enveloped them as they traversed the winding roads of St. Anne. The lush greenery of the island blurred past, a stark contrast to the grim puzzle awaiting them.

Mackenzie's grip on the wheel was steady, her knuckles betraying the tension she tried to conceal. Each turn brought them closer to the heart of the mystery, the unknown casting a long shadow over their shared destination.

As the salty breeze from the ocean teased through the slightly cracked window, a sense of foreboding hung heavy in the air. The rhythmic thud of the tires on the asphalt seemed to echo the beating of their determined hearts, ready to confront whatever secrets lay ahead at the scene of Jane Munro's disappearance.

Arriving at the crime scene, Paul glanced at the jungle path indicating fresh footprints. He knew his choice before the thought fully formed. This secluded isle fostered secrets worth unraveling, and he vowed to bring light where others saw only shadows.

As they approached, Paul studied the scene downshore, where more officers had arrived since Paul and Mackenzie made their appearance, though they seemed to be accomplishing very little. Overturned rocks and kicked sand revealed the extent of their search, which resembled children playing rather than police work.

The crime scene was situated at the juncture where the beach and jungle intertwined. The meeting of these two contrasting worlds seemed to amplify the unsettling aura of the place, as if nature itself held secrets waiting to be uncovered. The convergence of the serene shoreline and the untamed wilderness only added to the mysterious nature of the investigation, drawing Paul deeper into the heart of the mystery.

As Paul moved closer, Mackenzie was discreetly observing from a distance as he scrutinized the crime scene. Her presence, though unobtrusive, spoke volumes about her dedication to the case and her willingness to support the investigation in any way possible. Despite her initial reservations about Paul's involvement, Mackenzie's silent vigilance hinted at a potential ally in the pursuit of justice and truth.

A brief conversation caught his attention: the police chief instructing his men how to undermine leads before following them. Corruption was not new here, merely better concealed, its roots sunk deep into this community's soul. As Paul watched, boat engines roared and the crowd dispersed, the mission evidently completed.

Paul mumbled to himself that the police chief has held the chief title for far too long, a reign tainted with whispers of corruption since the beginning of his tenure. The stench of deceit seems to have followed him like a loyal shadow, casting doubt on every investigation under his watch.

All but two officers departed; these lingered in the shade chatting. One officer aimed furtive glances around as if fearful of watchers, bringing a hand to his ear, receiving new orders, no doubt. His partner paced anxiously.

Paul scrutinized their body language, piecing together more of the dysfunction of the local police under this crooked chief's control. Some sought truth, others preservation of their hold. But any seeking profit from another's agony would find Paul a formidable adversary, regardless of the price. His days of idleness ended now. This quiet paradise begged his aid, and he would not be deterred from service to the light of justice.

Moving among the local fishing crews readying their boats, Paul listened to fragments beyond the surface chatter. Yet all fell silent at his approach, eyes averted. These people endured years shrouded in mistrusting their neighbors' intents. One aged fisherman proved the sole exception. "Aye, heard about the girl," he said, tying off ropes. "Jane Munroe, help folks in need, if you follow. But she made enemies of those in power." Paul noted the subtle emphasis, and unease in those weathered eyes.

"Enemies? How so?" The man shook his head. "Best not ask too much, sir. This place, it protects its own. Police already grow impatient to be done with this business." At that, he hurried off, leaving Paul to ponder the inference, official indifference stemmed not from incompetence alone. He had witnessed such behavior before, where authority served darker designs under the law's guise.

As cries of gulls accompanied his walk inland, fragments assembled into a disquieting mosaic. Something was rotten here beyond one missing woman, and lifting the shroud would demand his utmost skill and discretion. For here, shadows covered snugly over truths many would kill to keep hidden.

As the sun sank towards indigo waves, Paul moved closer towards the search perimeter. His practiced observations noted every sign that the efforts of the police lacked real purpose. Officers chatting idly instead of questioning villagers further, cursory glances at areas dense with clues rather than taking a warranted closer inspection.

One officer leaned against a palm tree, fingers tapping restlessly as his gaze drifted to distant sights. Boredom ill-suited to the stress of missing persons. Another spoke urgently into his radio, his face taut, yet his half-hearted sweeps resumed without pause.

Crouching, Paul scanned the scene with a detective's acuity. Minuscule details emerged that the untrained eye overlooked, scuffed foliage, snapped twigs, scrapes in the dirt. To him, these spoke volumes, painting a story at odds with the findings thus presented.

Subtle cues like tight shoulders and forced cheer hinted at unease greater than this sole incident. Years protecting their own had bred complacency and carelessness towards the people they purportedly served. Such corruption festered in darkness; its spread prevented solely by people of conscience willing to stand in the gap.

Rising with a sigh, Paul knew his part had just begun. For justice to prevail here, full light must be shed upon the truths such oppressors sought to hide away in this place's shadowy corners. His long retrospect was ended; the game had only just begun.

Paul decided to come back later for another look around the crime scene. He walked to Officer Mackenzie and asked her to drive him home.

On the way back to Paul's, he asked Mackenzie what her impression of the crime scene was. "At first, I was concerned and curious when I surveyed the crime scene. The signs of struggle and the subtle inconsistencies were puzzling," she admitted.

Paul made a mental note that she seemed to be hinting at a deeper complexity beyond a mere accident. Her sharp eye for detail and her instinct for detecting deception likely raised questions in her mind about the true nature of the crime. He knew Mackenzie, and knew as she delved deeper into the investigation, she would have an increased sense of wanting to uncover the hidden truths lurking beneath the surface of this perplexing case.

That evening, after Mackenzie dropped Paul off at his bungalow, the last glimmers of sunlight faded from the west. Paul gathered his materials and set out to revisit the crime scene.

His night vision goggles had proven invaluable in the past. With the moonlight staining the jungle silver, he found irregularities abundant. Scuff marks at the crime scene were disguised, disturbances smoothed over. Someone wanted the truth unread. Scanning the undergrowth, flashes of metal caught his gaze. Tucked within leaves lay a broken necklace, its medallion unique.

As Paul revisited the crime scene under the cloak of night, the eerie stillness of the surroundings amplified the gravity of the situation. The moon's feeble glow cast elongated shadows over the area, obscuring and revealing in equal measure. Every step taken felt like a deliberate dance with danger, yet he pressed on, fueled by an insatiable thirst for the truth.

His eyes scanned the scene meticulously, noticing subtle signs of disturbance that daylight had attempted to mask. The faintest impressions in the soil, a glint of something metallic catching the moonlight, it all painted a different picture from the one officially portrayed.

The question that gnawed at Paul like a persistent itch was why the local police seemed determined to sweep these crucial clues under the rug. What were they hiding, and more importantly, who were they protecting by obscuring the truth? The realization that the very upholders of justice might be complicit in a cover-up filled him with a mix of anger and grim determination to unearth the buried secrets.

Stepping from within the shadows, Paul breathed deep, dew-laden air, his senses aglow with purpose. He knew Jane's disappearance was not a simple kidnapping. He knew there was something more going on here. Much more.

The following morning, stepping onto his porch as dawn lit the east, Paul sank into his weathered chair with a sigh. With his hands clasped, he analyzed in his mind the findings from last night's visit to the crime scene, all while the jungle awoke around him.

This was no mere missing person case, but a knotted web whose strands interlaced with those oppressing the local people. Who had cause to hide Jane's disappearance, and how far would they go to contain the ripples her absence caused?

His retirement's calm proved more fiction with each turning of events. Though he'd walked this land in peace, its wounds now bled afresh and demanded satisfaction. How could he ignore the call, when consciences grew silenced and the vulnerable had none to amplify their cries?

As the morning sun continued to rise, the shroud of mystery from the crime scene ignited a fire within Paul, a flame fueled by injustice and the shadow of deceit that loomed over Jane Munro's disappearance. The insidious web of lies and cover-ups spun by powerful hands on this island gnawed at his conscience, igniting a spark of righteous indignation.

It was not just the glaring inconsistencies and buried truths that compelled him to take on this case; it was the voiceless plea for justice echoing in the silence of the night. Jane Munro, a nameless enigma to many, held a significance that transcended mere mysteries. She represented every victim overlooked, every truth stifled, and every cause forsaken in the name of corruption.

Solving this case became a personal crusade against the darkness that threatened to engulf Paul's paradise. It was about standing up to those who wielded power as a shield for their misdeeds, about unmasking the perpetrators and giving a voice to the voiceless.

For Paul, solving this case wasn't just an option; it was a moral imperative, a chance to uphold the eroded pillars of justice in this island community.

With dawn's light, Paul set out determinedly.

First was a discreet visit to Mackenzie, requesting files under the guise of offering insight from experience. To reach Mackenzie's place, Paul took a leisurely 30-minute stroll along the winding paths that led to her quaint residence on the outskirts of town.

Nestled among the lush greenery of St. Anne, her home exuded a sense of quiet serenity, a stark contrast to the tumultuous events unfolding in their investigation. The walk allowed him to clear his mind and focus on the task at hand, preparing to engage Mackenzie in their collaborative pursuit of truth and justice.

Abigail 'Abby' Mackenzie's house reflected her practical and no-nonsense nature. It was a modest yet well-kept home, with a cozy charm that welcomed visitors. The exterior boasted vibrant flowers lining the pathway to the front door, adding a touch of color to the serene surroundings.

Inside, the furnishings were simple and functional, with a few personal touches that hinted at Mackenzie's personality. The ambiance was warm and inviting, a sanctuary amidst the chaos of their investigations, where they could strategize and collaborate in their pursuit of truth.

As Paul approached Mackenzie's house, the weight of the pending investigation seemed to hang heavier on his shoulders with each step. The morning air carried a sense of urgency, a silent call to action that resonated within. Knocking on her front door, he felt a strange mix of anticipation and apprehension swirling in his chest.

The hollow sound of his knuckles meeting the solid wood echoed in the stillness of the early morning, a stark reminder of the mysteries waiting to be unraveled. Behind that door lay a young officer caught in the crossfires of corruption, a potential ally in this intricate dance of shadows and truth.

The resolve in his heart was unwavering, fueled by the flickering hope of justice that seemed so elusive in this small island community.

As the door creaked open, revealing Mackenzie's determined gaze, Paul knew that this alliance would be crucial in the battles ahead. Together, they would stand on the precipice of a storm, ready to face the tempest of deceit and uncover the buried secrets that threatened to consume them both.

"Officer Mackenzie," Paul began, nodding in her direction as she met his gaze with a hint of suspicion. "I need to access the case files regarding Jane Munro's disappearance. There are details that warrant a closer examination."

Mackenzie raised an eyebrow, her expression guarded. "Why the sudden interest, Paul?" Paul leaned forward, the weight of the case heavy on his shoulders. "Some mysteries just refuse to fade, Mackenzie. And this one," Paul paused, his eyes locking with hers, "this one demands answers."

There was a flicker of understanding in her gaze before she acquiesced with a solemn nod. "I'll get the files for you. But tread carefully, Paul. This island doesn't take kindly to poking around where shadows linger."

She complied without question, trusting his intent though unease lurked in her eyes.

Mackenzie led Paul to her living room, where the faint scent of jasmine lingered in the air, imparting a sense of serenity amidst the storm of looming revelations. They settled on the well-worn sofa, surrounded by shelves of carefully arranged books and mementos that spoke of her past.

As they delved into the files on Jane's disappearance, meticulously organized on the coffee table before them, one detail stood out like a beacon in the sea of information. A witness statement, hastily dismissed by the local authorities, painted a vivid picture of a suspicious figure lurking near the scene on the night of Jane's vanishing. The significance of this overlooked testimony sent a ripple of intrigue through Paul, highlighting the glaring gaps in the official investigation.

As Paul continued to pore over the contents, a nagging sense of incompleteness gnawed at the edges of his consciousness. Vital pieces of the puzzle seemed deliberately obscured, redacted, or simply missing. The absence of crucial timestamps, obscured locations, and the notable omission of certain individuals from the investigative scope hinted at a calculated effort to obfuscate the truth, a truth that he was determined to uncover, no matter the cost.

The signs of cover-up were subtle yet telling. The hasty conclusions drawn by the local authorities, the reluctance of townspeople to speak freely about Jane Munro's case, and the thinly veiled threats that crept into conversations with influential figures, all pointed to a concerted effort to sweep the truth under the rug.

The whispers of corruption that echoed through the corridors of power on St. Anne hinted at a deeper conspiracy at play, one that sought to protect its own interests at the cost of justice for Jane and closure for her loved ones. It was this insidious undercurrent of secrecy and manipulation that fueled Paul's suspicion that Jane's disappearance was indeed being covered up by those in positions of influence.

Leaving Mackenzie's, he said he would be in touch soon and thanked her for the files.

Upon returning home from Mackenzie's, Paul shed his comfortable attire for a more inconspicuous ensemble befitting the undercover venture he was about to undertake. He opted for a simple, well-worn pair of dark jeans, a nondescript gray T-shirt, and a weathered leather jacket that had seen its fair share of covert investigations.

With a baseball cap pulled low over his eyes and a pair of sunglasses to shield his piercing gaze, he transformed into just another face in the crowd, blending seamlessly into the fabric of the island.

The decision to disguise himself was born out of necessity, a cloak of anonymity necessary to navigate the intricate web of secrets and lies that permeated St. Anne. To extract the truths buried beneath layers of deception, Paul needed to move unseen, to observe without drawing unwanted attention. The locals, tight-lipped and wary, were more likely to open up to a stranger wandering the streets than to a retired detective poking his nose where it didn't belong.

In this guise, Paul aimed to slip past the barriers of mistrust and silence that shielded the community from prying eyes, gathering the elusive threads of information that would lead him closer to unraveling the dark tapestry of secrets surrounding Jane Munro's disappearance.

Upon arriving in the village, he engaged some of the locals in casual talk, noting flickers beneath their practiced disinterest. With gentle assurance, he drew out fears taut as bowstrings. Piece by piece, a fuller picture emerged, Jane assisting the needy, gathering evidence against corruption. Enemies made, thereby whispers of threatened retribution. Though threats of danger hung thick as the jungle air, Paul pressed on quietly gleaning fragments none wished to speak of openly.

He lingered in disguise well into the night, navigating the labyrinthine streets of St. Anne and engaging with the local villagers under the veil of anonymity. Hours slipped by unnoticed as Paul wove through the shadows, eliciting morsels of information and elusive truths from the reticent townsfolk.

The veil of disguise not only shielded him from recognition but also granted him access to the whispered confidences and guarded gestures that betrayed hidden truths. Each exchange, each fleeting glance, held a piece of the puzzle, a puzzle he was determined to solve, no matter how long it took.

The cloak of anonymity became his ally in the dance of shadows and secrets, an essential tool in his pursuit of justice for Jane Munro and the unraveling web of deceit ensnaring St. Anne.

His examinations uncovered what official efforts overlooked, or didn't want to see, a missing thread woven through with corruption, whose discovery could lift shrouding oppression from this land at long last. How could he stand idle, knowing justice and true peace were within reach if only darkness' veils were torn away?

Feeling exhaustion setting in, Paul started his walk home.

Gripping his mug, and sitting on the porch, Paul watched gulls play upon offshore currents, reconsidering paths which once seemed set. His skills required honing no longer; his experience alone could expose what many wished kept in secret.

This community's vulnerable sought an advocate, and if none stepped forward, none would. Rising determinedly, Paul began preparations for undertakings certain to stir the wrath of the powerful.

His retirement now ended; his role was to seek truth until it shone its light upon answers none wished unveiled.

This day, Paul's journey began anew, to lift oppression's shadow from a land yearning for the dawn.

CHAPTER TWO

Ripples of Unease

⁓

THE MORNING SUN ROSE OVER THE JUNGLE CANOPY, CASTING LONG shadows across the village. The sunrise on St. Anne is a magical sight, one of the main reasons Paul chose St. Anne as his retirement place of choice. The sky ablaze with hues of pink and gold, painting the clouds in a fiery dance. The jungle below awakens with a symphony of chirping birds and rustling leaves, as if nature itself is greeting the new day with open arms. The first rays of light pierce through the dense canopy, casting long shadows that slowly retreat as the sun climbs higher in the sky. It's a moment of tranquility and beauty amidst the chaos of his investigation.

Paul set out early, determined to gain more information about Jane and her last days on the island.

The sun played hide-and-seek behind wisps of clouds, casting intermittent shadows on the cobblestone streets. A warm breeze carried the scent of salt and frangipani, mingling with the bustling chatter of vendors setting up their stalls.

As he meandered through the marketplace, the weather seemed almost too perfect, a stark contrast to the unsettling mystery of Jane's disappearance weighing heavy on his mind. The incongruity of nature's serenity against the backdrop of a potential crime scene stirred a restlessness within Paul, fueling his determination to unravel the truth lurking beneath the island's tranquil facade.

The weather that morning, with its deceptive tranquility, served as a reminder of the duality of existence on St. Anne, beauty marred by hidden dangers. It sharpened his senses, pushing him to delve deeper into the shadows cast by the sun, knowing that sometimes, the darkest truths lurk behind the brightest facades.

Paul started by casually chatting with vendors as they prepared their stalls for the day. The market was a lively tapestry of colors and sounds. Stalls filled with exotic fruits and freshly caught fish lined the narrow pathways, their vibrant hues contrasting with the muted tones of weathered wooden structures. The air was perfumed with the scent of spices and ripe produce, enticing passersby to stop and sample the local delicacies.

Locals bartered energetically, their voices blending with the clinking of coins and the rustling of palm leaves in the gentle breeze. It was a bustling hub of activity, a microcosm of island life where stories and secrets intertwined amid the daily commerce.

Most vendors were tight-lipped at his questions, giving curt answers before changing the subject. A few claimed to not know Jane at all. As Paul pressed further, some added they hadn't seen her in weeks. It was clear her disappearance made them uncomfortable.

After leaving the market, Paul walked the dirt paths between thatched-roof huts, knocking politely on doors. The few villagers who answered insisted they knew nothing helpful. One elderly woman nervously said she hoped Jane was found safe, before quickly closing her door.

The dirt paths winding between the huts on St. Anne paint a vivid picture of the island's raw authenticity. The huts, with their thatched roofs weathered by sun and sea spray, stood stoically against the elements. Some were adorned with vibrant bougainvillea climbing their walls, adding a touch of color to the earthy surroundings.

The yards surrounding the huts varied from meticulously tended gardens bursting with tropical blooms to barren patches of dust where resilient weeds persevered. Laundry fluttered on lines strung between coconut palms, and the scent of spices and smoke lingered in the air from distant hearths.

Dogs lounged lazily in the shade, flicking their ears at passersby, while children played barefoot in the dirt, their laughter a melodic backdrop to the island tapestry.

As Paul walked those dirt paths, he observed the inhabitants going about their daily routines. Women in bright sarongs haggled over fruits and fish at makeshift stalls, their laughter carrying on the breeze. Men repaired fishing nets under the watchful gaze of elders seated in the shade, swapping stories of bygone days.

The palpable sense of community hummed in the air, weaving a rich history of island life that both fascinated and comforted Paul in its simplicity and complexity.

Each hut bore witness to the joys and sorrows of its occupants, their lives etched into the very fabric of the humble dwellings. The setting of those huts, with their weathered exteriors and vibrant interiors, whispered tales of resilience and unity, reminding him that amidst the mystery of Jane's disappearance, the heart of St. Anne beat strong with the spirit of its people.

By midday, Paul's subtle inquiries had turned up more questions than answers. He took a seat in the shade to ponder his next move. Though the heat bore down, a cool unease had settled over the community. Wherever Jane was, people feared speaking of her for reasons Paul was determined to uncover.

He decided to wait until the sun went down and the temperatures cooled before continuing his investigation. The sun was unforgiving, its harsh rays beating down relentlessly on Paul's shoulders as if daring him to waver in his pursuit of the truth. The heat wrapped around him like a suffocating blanket, pressing down with its oppressive weight, making every step feel like a battle against the elements.

Sweat beaded on Paul's brow, trickling down his back as he navigated the crowded market, his senses sharp despite the discomfort. It was a reminder that on St. Anne, even the sun conspired to test one's resolve.

Having little success with the locals answering his questions, Paul began focusing his efforts on those in power.

Paul made a decision to focus the investigation on the mayor, a decision which stemmed from a keen understanding of the power dynamics at play on St. Anne. The mayor, Richard Harris, exuded influence that extended like tendrils into every corner of the island's operations. From shady dealings to whispered rumors of corruption, his name was a shadow cast over the very fabric of the St. Anne community.

Choosing to start with the mayor was a strategic move born out of necessity. In a place where secrets whispered on the breeze could spell danger, Paul knew that unraveling the mystery of Jane's disappearance would require confronting the source of that power, the man who held the strings of authority and control.

Moreover, his instincts as a seasoned detective sharpened by years of solving intricate cases honed in on the mayor as a pivotal figure in this unfolding drama. The pattern of events, the subtle nuances in conversations, the shoddy police investigation, and the lingering glances exchanged in the marketplace all pointed to the mayor's potential involvement, or at the very least, his knowledge of crucial information surrounding Jane's disappearance.

Delving into the dark heart of authority was a risky endeavor, fraught with peril and uncertainty. Yet, Paul's unwavering commitment to seeking justice for the vulnerable, for those whose voices were silenced by fear and intimidation, fueled his resolve to confront the mayor head-on. In a world where power often shielded the guilty and obscured the truth, he knew that unraveling the mayor's role in this mystery was an essential step towards shedding light on the shadows that threatened to engulf St. Anne.

Paul suspected there was more to Mayor Harris than met the eye, especially with the rumored connections to the missing person case. He needed to gather evidence discreetly to see if there was a link between him and Jane Munro's disappearance. It's all about connecting the dots, and sometimes those dots lead to unexpected places. So, in a daring, but necessary move, Paul decided to pay the mayor a visit.

After dusk, he stealthily made his way to the edge of the mayor's property. The property exuded an air of opulence and power, set apart from the modest dwellings of the islanders. A tall wrought-iron gate marked the entrance, hinting at the exclusivity within. The driveway wound through lush gardens manicured to perfection, leading to a grand mansion that stood as a testament to wealth and influence.

The house itself was a stately two-story structure, with imposing pillars and ornate balconies overlooking the sea. Its facade gleamed in the sunlight, a facade that belied the darkness of the secrets within. Security cameras discreetly positioned hinted at a watchful eye, a stark contrast to the serene beauty of the surroundings. It was a fortress cloaked in luxury, guarding its mysteries with a facade of elegance.

The mayor's lavish lifestyle and affluent residence raise questions about the source of his wealth. It seems incompatible with his official salary and public position, hinting at potential illicit activities or undeclared income streams. Such extravagant properties often mask a darker truth beneath the facade of respectability.

Paul thought the mayor's wealth was entwined with corruption and exploitation, allowing him to maintain his luxurious lifestyle at the expense of others. It's a common tale in the world of power and politics, where appearances deceive, and wealth conceals a web of deceit.

Through the dense foliage, he watched with growing intrigue. Late into the night, strange visitors met with the mayor under the cover of darkness. Quick, hushed conversations were had. With his years of experience, Paul read furtive body language as more than mere political dealings.

One man in particular caught Paul's attention. He recognized the uncouth individual as a criminal long protected by corruption. As the man loaded something into his truck, Paul strained to get a better view. Whatever secrets were being exchanged, they confirmed his suspicions of deeper wrongdoing.

By the last visitor's departure, Paul had seen enough. The mayor's questionable alliance and cover of nightfall spoke of culpability, not innocence. Paul now had targets to investigate further. He would uncover what shadows of crime hid within this town's halls of power.

Alone, the mayor exited his home, entered his car, and drove off. Paul cautiously tailed him through town. Weaving between buildings, he tracked the mayor to a secluded warehouse. The warehouse was tucked away near the edge of the island, hidden in the overgrown foliage. It had a worn metal roof, walls streaked with rust, and a heavy padlock guarding its entrance like a fortress.

Inside, shadows danced in the dim light filtering through cracked windows, revealing rows of stacked crates and a musty scent of secrecy.

Peering through cracks in the door and walls, Paul listened intently to a heated discussion. "We have to clean this up before it leads back to us," the mayor warned others gathered within. "One loose end is manageable, but two might raise suspicion."

A gruff voice replied, "You assured me the first would be the end of it. Now there's talk of another woman gone missing. Your 'cleaning' isn't thorough enough."

The mayor seethed at the implication of fault. "I have this under control. Just take care of what must be done as discussed, and our problems disappear."

It seemed Paul had stumbled upon a meeting arranged in haste and fear. These were not the words of innocent men. He now knew without a doubt that Jane's fate related to corruption, and her disappearance was no mere accident. Paul had his first solid lead to pursue the truth hidden within these shadowy dealings.

Later that same evening, with the moon shrouded by clouds, Paul decided to visit the police station after leaving the mayor's house, a decision driven by a dual purpose, to gather vital information from official channels while navigating the murky waters of corruption that tainted law enforcement on St. Anne. The police station, once a symbol of justice and order, now harbored secrets and shadows that beckoned his scrutiny.

As he embarked on the drive to the police station, the moon shone brightly, casting a hue over the island's lush landscapes.

Paul made his way to the empty police station. The police station in St. Anne is a small building, small for a police station, that tries to exude authority but often falls short. It's a weathered structure, paint chipping off the walls, with a flickering neon sign that reads "St. Anne Police Department." As for why it's closed at night, that's a mystery that even the locals can't fully explain. Some say it's due to budget constraints, others whisper about strange happenings that make the officers avoid the night shift. But Paul had always thought there was a darker secret lurking in those shadowed halls.

Picking the lock took mere moments for his skilled hands. Inside, he shuffled quietly to the file room and located Jane's case. By flashlight, Paul read the reports, but something seemed off. Whole sections were stripped bare, pages removed, leaving gaping inconsistencies. Crucial witness testimonies and details of the crime scene were conspicuously absent. Someone had carefully altered the official record to craft a convenient narrative for the public.

It seemed his suspicions of a cover-up here ran deeper than expected. Paul now held damning evidence of corruption within this very institution of law and order. Nothing was as it seemed in this place, and powerful forces had much to hide about Jane's true fate. Whatever truth lay buried, Paul was more resolved than ever to exhume it. Flipping through lingering photos in the file, Paul gained a clearer picture of Jane.

Though an ordinary village woman, she had an inner strength and drive that troubled some. Jane worked closely with island charities and frequently reported on challenges facing locals. Paul noticed she kept thorough records of issues, undrinkable water, subpar housing, missing supplies, that never seemed to improve. Her passion to help others was admirable, but such advocacy also made powerful enemies. Jane had begun investigating the mayor's development projects and use of public funds. Paul pieced together what she knew of the corruption that was tightening its grip on the community.

It seemed Jane's good works helped the most vulnerable yet threatened those profiting from their struggles. Her disappearance now took on a new context of silencing dissent. Paul understood why so many feared the danger she uncovered and those willing to ensure it stayed hidden. Her fate was a warning, but her spirit kindled Paul's fire for justice.

Paul quietly exited the station into the moonlit streets. As he made his way back to his bungalow, a solitary figure caught his eye. Officer Mackenzie walking past the station with a haze in her eyes, as though her mind seemed elsewhere.

Paul called out softly, hoping for an open ear within the tainted force. Mackenzie spun, hand flying to her weapon until recognition took over. "What do you want?" she demanded, posture stiff with fatigue and worry.

Her reaction surprised Paul. Mackenzie's sudden withdrawal from the case raised Paul's suspicions. The pressure from her superiors might have played a role in steering her away from the truth they were trying to unravel. Corruption runs deep in these parts, and not everyone has the courage to swim against the current.

Slowly, Paul raised his hands. "Only to share what I've learned. This case bothers you too, doesn't it?"

Mackenzie scowled but did not deny it.

Reading the doubts in her eyes, Paul pressed on. "I have evidence the police investigation was altered. If we work together, we can find the truth." Long moments passed as the woman evaluated Paul. Paul, however, remained calm under her scrutiny, radiating only a desire for justice.

At last, Mackenzie nodded. "Show me what you have." Paul had gained a tentative foothold, and the partnership began.

Politics and power often taint even the noblest of institutions. However, under the current mayor's rule, the darkness has spread like a festering wound, infecting not just the police department but the very core of the community. Uncovering the truth is like peeling back layers of deceit, revealing a rot that must be rooted out for justice to prevail.

Paul led Mackenzie to the quiet outskirts of town. By moonlight, he detailed the inconsistencies found among witness accounts and at the crime scene. She listened closely, arms folded tightly. When Paul revealed the missing case file pages, Mackenzie's stoic mask cracked in recognition.

"You saw it too, didn't you?" Paul asked gently. "Irregularities the others overlooked."

Mackenzie was silent for a long moment before conceding. "Yes, there were...strange things. Witnesses we were told not to contact. Evidence deemed irrelevant by my superiors. I started doubting our investigation was thorough."

"But I couldn't act on my suspicions alone," she added. "Not without endangering my career, or worse. You've given me more reason to believe this case deserves a second look."

Despite protocol, she was willing to help uncover what corruption sought to keep hidden from the islands' people. Together, they had a chance of discovering the elusive truth. Paul and Mackenzie stood in silence, weighing their choices in the dim light.

After some reflection, Mackenzie spoke. "I'll assist your investigation...unofficially. But you must be discreet, our lives could be endangered if our actions are uncovered."

Paul nodded solemnly. "I understand the danger and will take every precaution. With your help accessing files and locations, we have the best chance of finding what really happened to Jane."

Mackenzie paused, then offered her hand to shake on their risky agreement. For Jane, and for the truth, she said. "Let's get to work."

"Meet me tomorrow night at the abandoned quarry. There's much more to uncover, and I trust your instincts."

Mackenzie's eyes widened slightly, a spark of curiosity flickering within their depths before a mask of guarded professionalism settled over her features. "Why there, Paul?" she inquired, her voice tinged with a note of intrigue.

He could sense the wariness in her stance, the unspoken questions hanging between them like a delicate web waiting to be spun.

Paul met her gaze with a steady look, his eyes reflecting the fading light. "There are truths hidden in the shadows, Mackenzie. Secrets that seek the protection of darkness. I believe that together, we can uncover what others might wish to keep buried," he explained, his words carefully chosen, laden with the weight of unspoken truths.

Mackenzie hesitated for a moment, a subtle shift in her demeanor betraying a glimmer of unease mingled with determination. "I'll be there," she finally replied, her voice firm, a hint of a challenge underlying her words. "But remember, this island has its dangers, and not all truths are meant to see the light of day."

A silent understanding passed between them, a pact forged in the darkness of that fateful evening. As they parted ways, the promise of collaboration lingered in the air, a fragile thread binding them together in the face of looming shadows and whispered mysteries.

As the two parted ways under looming shadows, a sense of purpose and unease filled Paul in equal measure. At last, he had an ally within the force, but tread closer to corruption's secrets with each discovery. Despite the threats entangling this island community, he was determined to shed light on its darkness before further lives could be lost to the shroud of night.

Chapter Three

A Helping Hand

USING THE NIGHT SKY AS COVER, PAUL QUIETLY MADE HIS WAY through the dense jungle foliage toward their agreed meeting place, a small clearing near the abandoned quarry. As he neared the location, Paul became increasingly alert, scanning his surroundings for any signs of danger. Soon, the silhouette of Officer Mackenzie came into view.

"Any problems?" Paul whispered as he approached.

Mackenzie shook her head. "I don't think I was followed."

Paul recounted the clues he had uncovered so far: the missing sections from Jane's file and the suspicious meetings at the mayor's property. Mackenzie listened intently, her brow furrowed.

"The mayor is corrupt, no doubt about it. But he has this entire island under his thumb," she said, sharing insider details from the force that shed new light on Paul's findings. Three other activists had gone missing in the past year, their disappearances hastily categorized as accidents or oversights, with no real effort made to investigate.

"There's more rot here than anyone knows," Mackenzie admitted. "But speaking out would only endanger my family."

Paul understood her predicament and offered his protection, enlisting her discreet help tracking leads through official channels. Though their assignments kept them adversaries by law, a tacit alliance had formed against greater threats. Both sensed that justice would not come easily, but their shared desire to expose the island's corruption bound them to this dangerous path.

With solemn agreement, they parted ways under the starry sky, determined to lift the shadows darkening this tropical paradise.

The next morning, Mackenzie was summoned by her superior. "That retired detective is poking around where he doesn't belong," her captain growled. "Go keep an eye on him and put an end to his investigation."

Though wary, Mackenzie saw an opportunity. "Consider it done," she replied. If she was positioned close to Paul, she could aid his search discreetly while dissuading scrutiny from the force. Mackenzie paid Paul a visit later that day.

"Captain's orders, I'm to make sure you stay out of trouble," she said.

Paul tensed, unsure if he could trust her. "Relax," Mackenzie whispered, "I'm on your side. Just play along like I'm watching you."

Under this guise, Mackenzie began actively assisting Paul. She provided case files without raising suspicion and acted as a liaison in the community.

"The fishermen saw someone near the cove last night. I'll drive you there tonight to have a look," she said. At first, Paul was skeptical of any ties Mackenzie had to the corrupt force. But Mackenzie's in-depth knowledge proved invaluable, and her desire to uncover the truth seemed genuine. An unlikely bond of trust was formed between the two, all with the goal of serving justice for Jane and the others who went missing and exposing the rot beneath St. Anne's picturesque surfac

That evening, under the guise of monitoring Paul's activity, Mackenzie drove them to the coastal area where Jane was last seen. Her jeep, a rugged beast as dependable as the tides, was a sturdy olive-green Wrangler, battered by sun and salt from the island roads. Mackenzie handled it like an expert, steering with a sure hand that spoke of countless miles driven in pursuit of justice. She navigated the twisting coastal roads with caution and determination, which

Paul equated to her character.

Paul surveyed the still roped-off scene with a keen eye. "See here," he pointed to traces of disturbed sand. "And here, the undergrowth shows signs of being trodden recently."

Mackenzie saw only an empty shoreline, but Paul's observation skills shone through. Deeper in the foliage, Paul knelt to examine something in the dirt. "These markings weren't made by animals. Someone struggled here and was dragged in that direction."

He led Mackenzie further until they came upon a hidden cove. "Look at the scrape on that rock, the dent in the tree trunk. A violent encounter occurred here, but the police search barely extended this far." Paul reconstructed the scene in vivid detail, while Mackenzie realized how much had been overlooked.

By the time they returned to the jeep, the fullness of night had fallen. Paul had established that Jane's disappearance was no random act, and the subsequent investigation nothing but a sham. Mackenzie felt a surge of determination to see the truth unveiled, no matter what the forces that tried keeping it buried.

Her allegiance to Paul's mission deepened as they drove back to Paul's bungalow under the moonlight, united in the pursuit of justice.

As they walked along the shore near Paul's bungalow in silence, Mackenzie's mind raced with all she had witnessed. She had studied that same scene for clues yet missed everything Paul had uncovered with but a glance. His observational skills were like nothing she had seen before.

Stealing a sideways look at Paul, Mackenzie felt a grudging respect take root. Though retired, this man remained as sharp and tenacious as any detective in his prime. "I underestimated you," she conceded. "My department doesn't have anyone half as good."

A faint smile played on Paul's lips, as if enjoying the rare praise. "I'm just looking closer than most."

"This place needs someone who will," Mackenzie nodded slowly. Maybe with his help, justice could be found for Jane and the others.

Once inside Paul's bungalow, they decided to begin covert surveillance on the mayor and his associates this coming weekend. Using skills honed from peers on the force, and her laptop which she retrieved from her Jeep, Mackenzie tapped into security cameras and police frequencies to monitor their movements.

As Mackenzie revealed her covert hack into the mayor's surveillance system, a thin smile tugged at the corners of Paul's lips. He couldn't help but admire her tenacity and resourcefulness, qualities that mirrored his own in his heyday as a detective. The dimly lit room enveloped them in an air of secrecy, the soft glow of the monitors casting a flickering light on their determined faces.

"Mackenzie, you've certainly taken a page out of the old detective playbook. Well done," he commended her, his tone laced with a hint of approval. "These glimpses into the mayor's activities might just be the key to unlocking the mystery surrounding Jane Doe's disappearance."

Mackenzie's eyes reflected a mix of apprehension and determination as she adjusted the screens, revealing shadowy figures moving in the mayor's office after hours. The truth was beginning to surface, piece by damning piece.

"I never pegged you as one to break the rules, Mackenzie. What made you decide to take this risk?" Paul inquired, always curious to understand the motivations driving her actions.

She met his gaze steadily, a flicker of defiance glinting in her eyes. "I couldn't stand by and watch injustice go unchecked, not when I have the means to uncover the truth. Someone has to hold these powerful figures accountable, and it might as well be us."

Their shared purpose in seeking justice for the downtrodden tied them together in this perilous dance with danger. The mayor's secrets were slowly unfurling before them, painting a grim portrait of corruption that ran deeper than they had anticipated.

Now that they had access to the mayor's security cameras and the police frequencies, they agreed to meet the next night to begin the covert surveillance. To remain unseen, Paul and Mackenzie predetermined their strategically placed hiding positions near the mayor's house, choosing to conceal themselves behind dense foliage near the property, using the cover of night to their advantage.

They communicated in hushed tones, relying on hand signals and a shared understanding of each other's movements to minimize any chance of exposure. The tension in the air was palpable as they waited for any sign of suspicious activity. Despite the stillness of the night, every creak or rustle seemed amplified, sending a chill down Paul's spine. Mackenzie's alertness and quick thinking made her a valuable partner in this delicate operation. It was a test of patience and nerves, knowing that one wrong move could jeopardize their entire investigation.

The adrenaline rush of that first stakeout with Mackenzie, the thrill of the unknown lurking just beyond the shadows, fueled Paul's determination to unravel the layers of deceit surrounding them. It was a defining moment that solidified their cautious camaraderie in the face of dangerous adversaries.

On the first night of surveillance, they witnessed the mayor's henchmen dumping equipment and documents in the swamp and meetings with known criminals, envelopes changing hands. Each new clue strengthened Paul and Mackenzie's certainty that corruption ran far deeper than one missing woman.

After several stakeouts, Paul began connecting disparate threads into an ominous tapestry. He shared his theories with Mackenzie, who offered valuable context to support the emerging picture of money laundering, drug running, and collusion with gangs to undermine opposition.

The conversation where Paul shared his theories with Mackenzie took place at his bungalow, in Paul's mind the safest place to meet. As the warm air surrounded them on the front porch, over-looking the beach, they huddled together, their voices hushed in the stillness of their meeting, just in case someone unseen might be listening.

"I've been connecting the dots, Mackenzie, and the picture that's emerging is far from pretty," he began, his words carrying the weight of the revelations he was about to unveil. "Jane Doe's disappearance isn't just a case of a missing person; it's a tangled web of deceit and power plays orchestrated by those in the highest echelons of influence on this island."

Mackenzie's brow furrowed in silent contemplation as she leaned in, eager to hear the details of his deductions.

"It all leads back to the mayor, Mackenzie. His late-night meetings, the erasure of evidence at Jane's hiding spot, the warning signs we've encountered, everything points to a well-orchestrated cover-up," Paul continued, each word carefully chosen to convey the gravity of the situation. He paused, letting the weight of his words settle between them before pressing on. "My theory is that Jane stumbled upon something she shouldn't have, something that threatened to expose the corruption festering at the core of this island. And those involved were willing to go to great lengths to silence her permanently."

Mackenzie's eyes widened with realization, a spark of determination lighting up her features. "So, what's our next move, Paul?"

He met her gaze, his own resolve unyielding. "We follow the trail, Mackenzie, wherever it may lead. We confront the darkness that lurks beneath the surface of this island and shine a light on the truth, no matter the risks we face." And with that shared understanding between them, the stage was set for their daring pursuit of justice within the looming shadows of deception that threatened to engulf them.

"It seems we've only scratched the surface," Mackenzie murmured grimly.

Paul nodded. "Who knows what other rot lies below this island paradise? Our mission has grown past one case into exposing an entire criminal enterprise. It will take all our skill and coordination to succeed against such powerful enemies."

As they prepared to part ways at dawn, a renewed determination toughened both their resolve. They had each other's trust, as well as the vital pieces of the puzzle. Now it was only a matter of completing it before the mayor's web of deception ensnared them for good. They bid farewell, each to their own home to shower, eat, and get some sleep, with the promise of meeting again the next day.

After parting ways with Mackenzie, Paul found himself navigating the delicate balance between preparation and reflection in the solitude of his humble abode. Once the beginning light of dawn had settled over the island, Paul retreated to his front porch, his haven shielded from the chaos that lurked beyond the walls of his home. The rhythmic crash of waves against the shore provided a soothing backdrop to his thoughts as he settled into his routine that bridged the gap between action and contemplation.

He took a moment to savor a simple meal he had prepared, the taste of the island's fresh produce mingling with the weight of the secrets he carried. Each bite was a fleeting respite from the turmoil that awaited him under the cloak of night.

As the morning progressed, he indulged in a brief yet refreshing shower, the warm water washing away the grime of the day's revelations. The steam enveloped him, a gentle shroud that offered a temporary reprieve from the pressing mysteries that demanded his attention.

With a clear mind and a renewed sense of purpose, he turned to the stack of weathered detective novels that lined his shelves. The familiar tales of cunning investigators and unsolved crimes provided a momentary escape, a reminder of the intricate dance between truth and deception that defined his life.

Lost in the pages of fiction, his thoughts drifted to the complexities of the case at hand. Each character, each subtle clue held a mirror to the shadows that loomed over St. Anne, a reminder of the stakes at play in his relentless pursuit of justice.

And as the day progressed, morning waned into the quiet embrace of early afternoon, Paul found comfort in the knowledge that each moment of respite brought him closer to the answers that awaited him in the darkness of the coming night.

Using his ceiling fan on high, Paul climbed into bed, hoping sleep would come easy, giving him a break from the tropical heat. It did.

As he embarked on the treacherous path back to the mayor's house that evening for another night of surveillance, a shroud of anticipation cloaked his every move. Under the veil of dusk, he navigated the winding paths that led him to the mayor's residence. Each step was a calculated dance between stealth and determination, his senses attuned to the slightest rustle in the shadows that threatened to betray his presence.

The cool night air whispered secrets of the island, a chilling reminder of the dangers that lurked in the darkness. His pulse quickened with every passing moment, the weight of the unknown pressing down on him like a leaden cloak.

Thoughts of Jane Munro, her fate intertwined with the shadows that enveloped him, haunted his every step. The urgency of uncovering the truth, of shining a light on the malevolent forces at play, fueled Paul's resolve like a blazing inferno in the cold expanse of the night.

Concerns loomed on the horizon like storm clouds gathering in the distance. The mayor's machinations, the threats that loomed over those who dared to defy him, cast a long shadow over his mission. Yet, within the uncertainty and peril, a singular truth rang clear: he could not falter in his pursuit of justice, no matter the cost.

As he drew closer to the mayor's estate, the imposing silhouette of his residence loomed against the starlit sky like a fortress besieged by shadows. With each passing moment, the weight of the night pressed down on him, a palpable reminder of the risks that lay ahead.

As he approached the threshold of the mayor's domain, a sense of grim determination settled over Paul, steeling his resolve for the challenges that awaited. The whispers of the night beckoned him onward, a solitary figure bound by duty and driven by the unwavering pursuit of truth amidst the veils of darkness that enveloped St. Anne.

After an hour of watching, Paul tailed the mayor's men as they made another suspicious delivery. But as he tracked them through the jungle, Paul stepped on a fallen branch, the sharp crack like a gunshot in the dense silence. He dashed for cover but heard shouts approaching. Crouching low, Paul watched as flashlights slithered closer, holding his breath. At the last moment, a boar crashed noisily through the brush, drawing the men away.

The brush with danger, the cold breath of betrayal at his heels, urged Paul to make a swift and calculated decision, an instinct honed by years of navigating treacherous waters in pursuit of justice.

As the mayor's men closed in on his concealed vantage point, the fleeting dance of shadows and whispers of imminent discovery jolted him to the core. The looming threat of exposure, of facing the full force of the corrupt forces that governed St. Anne, sent a sharp shiver down his spine.

With a heavy heart and a mind steadied by grim resolve, Paul made the reluctant choice to disengage, to slip back into the embrace of the night and retreat to the sanctuary of his home. The echoes of impending danger lingered in the shadows, a stark reminder of the thin line between unyielding determination and perilous folly.

The weight of unanswered questions, the specter of unseen adversaries lurking just beyond the veil of darkness, fueled his retreat. The decision to leave and regroup was not a sign of surrender but a strategic withdrawal, a tactical maneuver born of caution and tempered by the wisdom of experience.

With each step homeward carrying the weight of unseen threats and unresolved mysteries, Paul hardened himself for the trials that awaited in the depths of the night, knowing that the battle for justice on St. Anne had only just begun.

Shaken, Paul returned home, thanking the boar. He recounted the close call to Mackenzie, who grasped his shoulders fiercely.

"Dammit Paul, they'll kill you without a second thought! Promise me you'll be more careful." Her concern took him aback.

He met her gaze steadily. "I won't stop till we find the truth, no matter the risks."

Mackenzie sighed. "I know, just...don't do this alone anymore." Her admission of care touched him deeply.

"You're the only ally I have," he said quietly. "We face this threat together, till the very end."

A silent understanding passed between them. Their unlikely camaraderie had evolved into a partnership willing to defy any danger for justice's sake. And so, their investigation continued under cover of night, the solitary light in an island shrouded by corruption.

The following evening, Paul met Mackenzie in their usual remote meeting spot.

"We've come too far to back down now," he said resolutely.

Mackenzie nodded. "I'm with you all the way, though God knows what further dangers lie ahead. What's our next move?"

A steely glint entered Paul's eyes, mirroring her own. "Until Jane and the others find justice. I'll shed light on every ugly secret, no matter the cost."

Mackenzie gripped his arm. "Then the fight is ours. One way or another, we'll pull this island from the clutches of corruption together."

With a resolute nod, they parted to prepare for the clandestine mission ahead, more committed than ever to truth in the face of mounting threats.

Paul and Mackenzie discreetly finalized preparations for another search in the jungle, near the mayor's house. Paul listed the tools needed for their mission: lockpicks, flashlights, recording devices, and cameras to document any discoveries. Not since his active days did Paul feel such a surge of purpose mingled with peril.

His steady gaze met Mackenzie's resolute one. "We do this right and get out fast." If their activities were exposed prematurely, all hope of truth and justice could be lost.

The air was tense between Mackenzie and Paul. They shared a silent understanding as they readied for their mission, knowing what lay ahead. There was a mix of apprehension and steely determination in their eyes, a silent agreement to delve into the heart of the mystery despite the risks. Mackenzie's resolve mirrored Paul's, a shared sense of purpose that drove them forward into the unknown.

With a final nod, they slipped into the black night, each returning to their respective homes.

Unknown to the looming threats, St. Anne's only beacon of justice gathered momentum underground. Paul and Mackenzie's crusade advanced further into shadowy terrain. Yet their determination to lift the veil of deception remained unfaltering, come what may.

After parting ways with Mackenzie following their planning session for the upcoming search of the jungle area near the mayor's house, Paul returned home.

The first thing he did upon entering was secure all points of entry, ensuring his sanctuary remained safe from prying eyes or unwelcome intruders. The events of the day lingered in his thoughts, swirling like a storm waiting to unleash its fury.

Settling into his routine before bed, Paul took a moment to review the clues and information gathered so far, organizing them meticulously in his ever-present trusty notebook. Each detail was a piece of the puzzle, a clue waiting to be deciphered.

He made sure to double-check their plans for the next day's search, mapping out the area near the mayor's house in his mind, anticipating any obstacles or hidden dangers that may lie in wait.

Before retiring for the night, he took a few moments to meditate, letting the gentle rhythm of his breath calm the storm of thoughts swirling within. It was essential to clear his mind, to focus on the task at hand without distractions or doubts clouding his judgment. With a renewed sense of purpose and determination, Paul finally settled in for a night's rest, knowing that tomorrow would bring new challenges and revelations in their relentless pursuit of the truth.

CHAPTER FOUR

Following the Trail

USING THE DARKNESS OF NIGHT, AND THE FACT THAT THE POLICE station would be empty, Paul and Mackenzie entered the front lobby of the station using a key Mackenzie had 'borrowed' from another officer. No need for Paul to pick the loch this time.

They quickly made their way to the file room to make one more search of Jane's file. Rummaging through the filing cabinets, Paul came across Jane's journal tucked in the back of one of the lower drawers. Obviously hidden from prying eyes. While looking through case files in search of a missing witness statement, something caught his eye. Nestled between folders labeled "Cold Cases" was a dusty leather-bound journal, its cover slightly worn from age.

Drawing it out from its hidden spot, Paul could sense the weight of its potential significance. Opening it revealed pages filled with cryptic symbols and peculiar markings. His detective instincts immediately kicked in; this was no ordinary journal. It was a treasure trove of information waiting to be deciphered.

As he carefully examined each page, the pieces started falling into place. There was a pattern to the chaos, a method behind the madness. Jane had cleverly concealed vital information within the coded messages, and it was up to Paul to unravel the mystery.

The journal held the key to unlocking the truth behind Jane's disappearance, and he was determined to see it through.

"Mackenzie, take a look at this," Paul said, holding up Jane's journal open to a particularly convoluted page.

Mackenzie wrinkled her forehead, examining the jumble of letters and symbols. "Looks like some kind of code."

"Exactly," he replied, tapping the page with his pen. "I believe this journal holds the key to uncovering Jane's secrets. We need to decode it to find the location of that secret meeting she mentioned."

Mackenzie nodded, her eyes reflecting determination. "So, what's the plan, Paul?"

"We head to the jungle," he stated matter-of-factly. "I have a hunch that the meeting spot is hidden within the greenery. We'll need to keep our wits about us and be prepared for anything. Let's not waste any time. Time to put our detective skills to the test."

"The mayor's house will have to wait, for now."

Before leaving the police station, they were careful to replace everything they touched to its original location. As the shadows cast their veil over the station, they stealthily made their exit, shrouded in the cloak of darkness. The night was their ally, concealing their movements as they slipped out unnoticed by prying eyes.

With the journal clutched securely in Paul's hand, they ventured into the black night, the city's hum fading into the distance. The faint glow of lampposts guided their path as they navigated the labyrinthine streets toward the outskirts of town.

The jungle beckoned, its secrets waiting to be unearthed.

Silent communication passed between them, a shared understanding of the gravity of the mission. Step by step, they drew closer to the dense foliage that concealed the mysteries they sought to unravel. The night air was thick with anticipation, each rustle of leaves and a whisper of wind propelling Paul and Mackenzie forward on their quest for truth.

Once in the dense jungle, they were guided only by the light of their flashlights, searching for any signs of the secret meeting spot hinted at in Jane's coded journal. The jungle was eerily quiet except for the occasional hoot of an owl or rustle of nocturnal creatures in the undergrowth.

After half an hour of careful trekking, they came upon a small clearing sheltered by towering mahogany trees. Overgrown vines and ferns partially obscured a crudely constructed wooden shelter tucked away in the shadows.

Paul signaled for Mackenzie to hold position as he cautiously approached the rudimentary structure. Peering inside, he saw remnants of a camp, a burnt-out fire pit, a smashed lantern, and a torn canvas. But it was the contents scattered among the debris that caught his eye. They entered cautiously.

Papers bearing Jane's handwriting along with financial ledgers and photo evidence of corrupt dealings. It seemed this had been Jane's base of operations in her pursuit of the truth. Motioning Mackenzie over, they began sifting through the treasure trove of clues by flashlight.

Paul's keen eye noted coded notations that warranted further examination along with names and places of interest. It appeared Jane was close to exposing a web of money laundering, graft, and criminal alliances reaching the highest levels of power.

Paul shined his flashlight on the documents, scanning for any detail that could further their investigation. A symbol caught his eye, it appeared to be a code representing illegal shipments.

As they sorted through the debris, Mackenzie stumbled upon a tattered notebook buried under litter. Its pages contained disturbing references to dangerous figures and alluded to Jane believing her life was in jeopardy. Flicking to the final entry, a chilling phrase made their blood run cold: "They're coming for me now."

A snapping twig in the distance cut the night like a knife. Paul doused his light and tugged Mackenzie into the darkness just as shadows closed in on the clearing. Had they been followed? Were the mayor's men now on their trail? Crouching low below the windows, Paul and Mackenzie peered out at three shadowy figures cautiously approaching the clearing. Two carried flashlights while the third brandished a tire iron, clearly searching for intruders. As the beam swept over where they'd been moments ago, Paul's grip on his pistol tightened.

Once the figures moved on, the pair slipped ghost-like through the dense foliage, tracking the interlopers' path. Soon, they came upon signs of struggle, deep gouges in the soft earth, and torn ferns stained black. Following the erratic trail, more clues were unearthed. A discarded flashlight, its lens smashed. Shredded notepaper bearing Jane's hand. A lone shoe caked in dried blood.

The trail led to a steep ravine where the moonlight failed to penetrate. But Paul's keen eyes spotted something wedged between rocks near the edge. Scaling down with care, he retrieved a tattered scarf that Mackenzie recognized as Jane's favorite. There were no further tracks to follow, yet the evidence they'd found painted a grim picture.

Jane had clearly been waylaid here in a brutal abduction, likely by the very men they'd been tracking. And now it seemed those faceless enemies were on the hunt, intent on covering their crimes. Paul and Mackenzie had no choice but to retreat under cover of darkness, clutching the scant clues that might help locate where poor Jane met her fateful end. Paul and Mackenzie walked in tense silence as they traced their steps back through the dense undergrowth. Upon reaching the clearing once more, Paul withdrew a small digital camera from his pack.

Methodically, he photographed the clues they had discovered - the disturbed foliage, smears of blood, scattered papers - taking care to capture multiple angles that might provide new insights under scrutiny. Mackenzie watched with grudging admiration as his practiced eye gleaned every nuanced detail.

Back at his home, Paul spent hours poring over the images he had downloaded from his camera to his computer, enlarging and enhancing shots to pick out the minutiae his trained mind could process.

Slowly, a timeline unfurled before him. The gouges in the soft earth aligned with a struggle, feet dragging south towards the ravine. Bloody fingerprints on the demolished flashlight matched Jane's size. Shredded notes torn from a journal, the phrases out of order. A lone shoe pointed to an uneven gait as she was hauled away. By stitching together the fragments captured in light and shadow, Paul was able to reconstruct the harrowing sequence of events that dark night. It filled in gaps left by the corrupted police report and brought them one step closer to unmasking the evil orchestrating these devious acts.

Mackenzie, at her house, was able to get a few hours of sleep and began getting ready to leave to meet Paul once again. She found herself both bemused and impressed by Paul's insight. With his help, justice might prevail after all.

Paul forwarded via email one of the enlarged photos to Mackenzie, for her to inspect, highlighting a minute detail the police had overlooked. Faint zigzag indentations ran through the dirt, leading from the ravine into the undergrowth.

She was amazed at what Paul sees that no one else does.

Mackenzie arrived at Paul's home an hour later. Following Paul's earlier instructions, she had retrieved off-road vehicle reports from the station archives.

Scouring over the records, Paul's keen eyes noted suspicious inconsistencies. Several callouts to the logging camp aligned with their timeline but lacked proper documentation. A late-night call piqued his interest. The responding officers reported chasing off poachers in a truck. But their report was sloppy, the vehicle details scarce, almost as if it had been intentionally botched to hide the truth.

Studying photographs of the mayor's fleet, Paul matched tread patterns to the tracks at the scene of what was Jane's hideout. He was now certain the same four-by-four had been used in Jane's abduction. Its owner and the officers covering its crimes were the allies Paul suspected.

Since the police department managed all government vehicles

on St. Anne, Mackenzie agreed to inspect the mayor's vehicles under the guise of routine checks. With any luck, she might turn up new evidence from the vehicles and bring them one step closer to locating Jane.

For now, they had a valuable lead to pursue.

Under the murky glow of a crescent moon, Paul and Mackenzie decided to return to the jungle and settle into the dense bush bordering the remote logging camp owned by the mayor. They were drawn to the camp following a trail of clues intertwined with Jane's cryptic journal. It hinted at a clandestine meeting taking place within the depths of the camp, a meeting that could hold the answers they sought.

Once there, they'd witnessed sporadic comings and goings at the isolated compound, getting a feel for its strange rhythm. In the small hours, their vigilance was rewarded. A nondescript van rumbled to the heavy gates, which swung open sluggishly. Barely perceptible in the gloom, two hooded figures alighted and engaged in hushed dialogue with the guard, passing furtive packages between tense palms.

As the guard climbed into the van to offload his cargo, Paul edged closer through his camouflaged poncho, snapping shots with a long lens. Exchanging nods, he and Mackenzie memorized grainy glimpses of weathered faces and faded tattoos, possible leads in their search.

The guard hastily emerged, and the van's engine whined, fading into the night. They were on the verge of packing up when headlights stabbed through the dark, extinguishing any stars. Paul's breath caught in his throat. It was the same lumbering four-by-four he'd spied photos of earlier. The very vehicle that may have borne Jane to her fate. At last, their patience seemed poised to bear fruit.

The moment when Paul spotted the elusive four-by-four at the logging camp from the photo in his files, was a critical juncture in their investigation. The decision to further investigate or wait for a safer opportunity weighed heavily on Paul's mind.

Given the potential risks involved and the fact that they were already treading on dangerous ground, he chose caution over recklessness. It was vital to ensure their safety and avoid premature exposure that could jeopardize their pursuit of the truth. He signaled to Mackenzie it was time to go.

A sense of urgency and anticipation hung in the air like a thick fog. Every step they took was calculated, every glance over their shoulders a reminder of the shadows that lurked in the periphery. Paul and Mackenzie had carefully cataloged every detail observed, every whisper of suspicion that echoed in the stillness of the night.

As they made their way out of the jungle, Paul's thoughts raced with the possibilities and implications of their recent discoveries. The weight of responsibility for unraveling the mysteries that shrouded St. Anne pressed down upon him, urging Paul to stay vigilant and focused. It was a time of introspection and preparation, fortifying himself for the challenges that lay ahead in the relentless quest for justice.

The delicate dance between diligence and discretion.

The next day, Paul searched dusty records at the courthouse while Mackenzie ran background on the figures glimpsed at the logging camp. Pulling various threads together, their working theory was bolstered. The four-by-four and surrounding acres belonged to Evan Cole, a timber baron who had grown rich on island contracts. Further digging unveiled he was one of Mayor Harris's closest allies and funded several questionable political actions over the years.

More unsettling were murmurs of Cole's involvement in organized crime. Rumors of smuggling and ties to gangs on a neighboring island kept competitors fearful. It seemed the perfect camouflage for concealing more unseemly deeds underneath a legal veneer. Evan Cole was a man shrouded in shadows and suspicion. He is a wiry figure, with sharp eyes that miss nothing. His weathered face tells tales of a hard life, and his cautious movements hint at a man used to lurking on the edges of society. A tangled web of connections seemed to surround him, and uncovering his role in the unfolding mystery would only deepen the intrigue.

With Mackenzie's help recalling tattoos spotted on some of the suspects they have been tailing, Paul matched gang insignia to known felons in police databases. The men at the log yard were more than mere cronies. They were criminal players controlled by Mayor Harris and protected by Cole's wealth and influence on the island. All signs pointed to Cole being neck-deep in this corrupt enterprise. And if their hunch held weight, his sprawling property may currently hold the key to Jane's whereabouts and lifting the veil on the wider web of villainy strangling their tropical paradise.

Paul decided to return to the logging camp the next night for a more in-depth investigation. Mackenzie's voice held a hint of caution as they planned their next move.

She quietly remarked, "Are you sure about this, Paul? Breaking in could draw unwanted attention." Her words carried a weight of concern, a pragmatic reminder of the risks they faced in delving deeper into the shadows of the logging camp. But beneath her apprehension, Paul sensed a flicker of resolve, a readiness to follow him into the unknown despite the dangers that awaited them.

Paul turned to Mackenzie with a reassuring gaze, his tone firm yet comforting. "Trust me, Mackenzie," he said, "We tread carefully, watchful for any sign of trouble. Together, we'll navigate this path and uncover what's hidden in the shadows. Your courage matches your skill, and together we'll see this through."

Mackenzie's tense expression softened at Paul's words, a silent acknowledgment of the bond they shared in pursuit of the truth.

Under a new moon, Paul and Mackenzie cautiously made their approach to the logging camp. Mackenzie, ever the resourceful officer, concealed her vehicle in an old disused storage shed just off the beaten path. Guided by night vision goggles, they skirted the property, mapping blind spots and patrol routes before selecting an entry point.

With practiced precision, Paul picked the padlock securing a rear equipment shed. Inside, they discovered crates of smuggled goods and documents incriminating local politicians. Mackenzie photographed the haul while Paul scanned for any clue to Jane's fate.

A muffled cry from a different building in the distance sent their hearts racing. Slipping into the shadows, they observed two men drag a bound figure into a dilapidated structure. Though the identity was unclear, the victim's distress was real.

Once the men departed, Paul gestured for Mackenzie to keep watch. He crept towards the building, pulling out lock picks with steadied hands. Inside, he found Jane chained and bruised, but alive. Working fast, he freed her wounded body and offered comfort as best he could.

Footsteps approached again. Paul beckoned Mackenzie over their radio, hoping her skillful diversions could grant them safe passage out of this hell. With Jane in tow, they melted into the enveloping night, spirits lifted but dangers still lurking in the dark places they were uncovering.

Jane clung weakly to Paul as he helped her shuffle through the dense foliage. Behind them, clouds of gunfire choked the night, Mackenzie's diversion pulling heat from their escape.

As they cleared the tree line, Paul swept Jane into his arms and broke into a labored sprint. Mackenzie sped alongside in the four-by-four, its tailgate already flung down. In a seamless maneuver, Paul bundled Jane inside and vaulted up just as bullets shredded the bushes behind them. The jungle roads on St. Anne are as treacherous as they are narrow, especially when you're evading the mayor's unwelcome attention.

Mackenzie handled the twists and turns like a pro, her determination matching Paul's as they raced to safety through the dense foliage. The heat, the tension, and the pursuit only added to the thrill of the chase. Speeding towards the safety of Paul's bungalow, Paul assessed Jane's condition by flashlight. She was gravely dehydrated and covered in untreated wounds, but cognizant.

"You found me...thank you," Jane rasped, clutching Paul's hand with surprising strength. She detailed harrowing beatings at Cole's hands to uncover her sources before Paul interrupted gently.

"Rest now, you're safe." But Jane was determined. Reaching into a torn pocket, she produced a soiled notebook page. A list of names, places, dates, all connected to corruption on the island. "This is...what they wanted. Please, help the others." Then darkness claimed her once more. At long last, Paul held the missing piece, direct proof tying Cole to Jane's abduction and the island's secrets. The truth was theirs to wield at last.

Paul and Mackenzie had discovered crucial evidence at Cole's property that directly links him to Jane's abduction. Once at Paul's, he tended to Jane's injuries and started piecing together the significance of the evidence she provided.

CHAPTER FIVE

Phantoms in the Night

AFTER RETRIEVING JANE IN THAT HEART-POUNDING JUNGLE escape, Paul knew he had to ensure her safety before getting her medical help in the morning. They made a strategic stop at an abandoned fishing hut hidden along the coastline. The hut, weather-worn and secluded, provided temporary shelter for Jane as Paul and Mackenzie assessed her condition and tended to any immediate needs. The salty tang of the sea mingled with the musty scent of old wood within its walls, a stark contrast to the urgency of the situation.

The secrecy of their actions was paramount, every step taken was calculated to protect Jane and to keep their movements hidden from those who wished to silence them. It was a moment of respite in the chaos, a brief pause before the storm that awaited at the clinic.

In the morning, Mackenzie drove Paul and Jane to retrieve Paul's car from his house. Then, Paul drove Jane to a small clinic on the island, where the nurse could keep her safe and treat her in the short term.

The clinic was a rundown place, hidden away from prying eyes. It was like a forgotten relic, almost blending into the shadows. A place where whispers could easily get lost in the wind. The nurse had a tough demeanor that matched her shabby surroundings. She knew more than she let on. She was a no-nonsense woman with sharp eyes that seemed to size you up at a glance. Paul crossed paths with her a few times over the years, but he wouldn't share all his cards with her just yet. She has her own agenda, and it might not align perfectly with Paul's.

As for the nurse's loyalty and willingness to protect Jane, in the shadowy world of St. Anne's underbelly where alliances shift like sand, trust was a luxury Paul couldn't afford to give freely. He had to rely on his own wits and instincts to safeguard Jane's well-being. In the end, time would reveal whether the nurse would be a steadfast ally or a dangerous wildcard in the quest for justice.

After ensuring Jane was stabilized and protected, Paul returned home, his mind racing against all he had uncovered.

He decided to bolster the security in and around his home after the close calls he and Mackenzie had experienced in the jungle. Paul often felt there was more he could do to secure his home from intruders. He knew his enemies would be combing the island for any signs of him.

He installed new locks, reinforced weak points of entry, and set up motion sensors around the perimeter. He kept a vigilant eye out for any unexpected visitors. Normally, Paul was in awe of the morning sunrise, however, this morning it seemed to shed light on the dangers lurking in the shadows. It fueled Paul's determination to uncover the truth and make sure justice prevailed. After fortifying his bungalow, Paul spent most of the day reviewing his notes and clues, piecing together the puzzle that seemed to grow more complex by the hour.

With a cup of strong coffee in hand, and after checking on Jane's condition at the clinic, he immersed himself in the web of deceit that surrounded Jane's disappearance, determined to unravel it one thread at a time. As much as Paul yearns for a leisurely stroll along the beach or the gentle warmth of the Caribbean sun, duty calls louder than the siren song of paradise. While unraveling this intricate web of mysteries and deceit, his steps are guided by justice, not by the pleasures of a tranquil day.

With nightfall approaching, an eerie quiet fell over the jungle. Paul tried to relax with a book, but strange noises had him constantly on edge. His bungalow is a stone's throw away from the dense jungle that harbors secrets darker than the night itself. The proximity serves as a constant reminder of the thin line between tranquility and peril on this enigmatic island. Was it merely the normal sounds of nocturnal creatures in the forest, or were unseen eyes watching his property? Paul paced with growing unease, peering out into the encroaching darkness for any hints of movement.

The jungle on St. Anne is a realm of untamed beauty, shrouded in mystery and teeming with life. While it may lack conventional tourist attractions like botanical gardens or animal preserves, its rugged terrain offers adventurous souls the opportunity to explore hidden trails, discover exotic flora and fauna, and experience the raw vitality of nature in its purest form. However, in these verdant depths, one must tread cautiously, for the jungle keeps its own secrets, waiting to be unveiled by the bold and the brave.

As the hours passed, exhaustion pulled at his mind, but fear refused to let his body rest. Each snapping branch or rustling leaf had Paul's pulse quickening. He gripped his weapon close, mind racing with worries for Jane's safety and the escalating danger to himself and Officer Mackenzie. Sleep would not come easily in the shadow of the threats that now surrounded him on all sides. Only time would tell if his fortress would withstand the rising forces of corruption stalking the night.

He decided to follow a lead, a long shot lead, but still a lead. As for sleep that night Paul reasoned a safe roof over his head took a backseat to the urgency of the investigation. When duty calls, rest becomes a luxury one can ill afford.

As daylight broke, Paul, with no relief or rest, followed the lead to nowhere.

As the sun's rays filtered through the trees, he returned home and surveyed his property. He found the motion sensors had tripped! Approaching his door with caution, weapon in hand, Paul's worst fears were confirmed, the new locks had been broken, the door hanging ajar.

Stepping inside, Paul saw a scene staged to misdirect. Drawers and cabinets hung open, papers scattered across floors and tables.

Frowning, Paul studied patterns in the calculated chaos, realizing clues were being planted. A single bullet casing stood out to him, the make not matching his own weapons. And an amulet looped around a picture frame, one he recalled seeing hung around the neck of a known criminal associate of Evan Cole.

Paul realized his enemies sought to frame others for compromising his security, hiding their true involvement. They wanted Paul to distrust potential allies and chase dead ends. But their methods only cemented Paul's suspicion of Cole and the mayor.

Gathering a handful of clues, Paul cleaned and repaired the damage as swiftly as possible. The intruders wanted him fearful in his home, instead, their actions had the reverse effect, hardening Paul's resolve to maneuver freely without fear as the layers of corruption were peeled back one by one.

With his security breached, Paul knew it was only a matter of time before more drastic measures would be taken. He needed allies and a new strategy. After dark, Paul slipped into the jungle and made his way to the rendezvous point with Mackenzie.

"They're stepping up the threats," Paul told her grimly, recounting the staged break-in. Mackenzie listened with a frown, equally wary of escalating dangers.

"We need to move Jane, erase our trails in town," Mackenzie said. Paul nodded in agreement. Their safety, and truth itself, depended on evading any eyes and ears reporting to the mayor.

As Mackenzie and Paul put their heads together, plans were hatched for countering the looming threats. Mackenzie would discreetly relocate Jane to a hidden shelter, then spread misinformation that Jane had left the island among her contacts. Meanwhile, Paul would disappear off the grid for a time, using the jungle he knew so well to slip his followers unnoticed. When the time was right, they would cautiously continue peeling back the layers of corruption. But for now, going dark was the surest way to stay alive and free until the next moves could be made.

With renewed resolve, Paul and Mackenzie parted ways into the night, preparation for difficult days ahead fully underway.

After laying low for several nights, Paul emerged from the jungle into an abandoned shack deep in the forest, far removed from any prying eyes. The abandoned shack once belonged to an old fisherman who used to reside on the island. Paul had stumbled upon it during one of his late-night stakeouts. Sometimes the forgotten corners hold the most telling secrets Here, past the reach of the mayor's network, he hoped to uncover further clues undisturbed.

Rummaging through decaying papers and files left behind, Paul's hopes were realized. Hidden beneath the floorboards were tan-colored envelopes, their contents remarkably well-preserved. Paul pulled out sheaves of documents, land deeds, financial records, and even communications discussing schemes both legal and not. It seems this shack was not abandoned, rather, commandeered by the mayor's henchman.

As Paul scanned the material, he pieced together a more unsettling truth about the man pulling the island's strings. The mayor had long profited from manipulating the system to his advantage, engaging in bribery, and extortion, and using his office to enable other criminal ventures with a willful blind eye. Now the full scope of his corruption came into focus. Paul gathered the evidence of the mayor's past wrongdoings, knowing such leverage, in the right hands, might help deter further threats or obstruction. But first, he had to stay alive, keep peeling back the layers until the rotten core was fully exposed for the island to see at last.

Paul studied late into the night, and the pieces of the greater puzzle began falling into place. Jane's charities worked closely with victims of the mayor's schemes, she must have learned more than anyone realized. The documents Paul now held revealed enormities beyond what Jane first uncovered. Kickbacks, money laundering, names of protected criminal figures given free rein on the island.

Jane was pulling back the veil on a full-fledged criminal syndicate operating from city hall itself. Small wonder her abduction served as a chilling warning. Paul now understood she walked too close to secrets some would kill to keep hidden. And in exposing them, Jane signed her own death warrant and made herself a target in the ruthless game being played.

Paul's blood ran cold as he pondered Jane's brave search for truth on the island's behalf, ending in the worst way. But her efforts would not be in vain. Paul knew he must follow the trail she blazed, pick up the fallen banner, and use every clue to bring the shadows to light once and for all. For Jane, and all the others. The fight for justice was only beginning.

As night fell once more, Paul packed away the incriminating documents and slipped back into the cover of darkness. His mind raced against all that had been learned, and all that was still at risk should the mayor's true nature be revealed. A man who built an empire on the back of others' suffering and misfortunes would stop at nothing to maintain his grip on power. Paul suspected those who learned too much, like Jane, signed their lives away. And now he, too, danced on the edge of a blade simply by pursuing truth and justice.

What lengths would the mayor and his allies go to if cornered? Paul had tangled with corrupt figures before, and seen how ruthlessly they fought to preserve the shadows. With so much to lose now, there was no telling how far enemies would go to bury past sins. Paul readied himself as best he could, knowing the stakes had risen higher than ever before. To survive and win, he would need to outwit those who played for keeps. The game had entered its most dangerous phase, where one wrong step meant falling into the deep. But retreat was not an option, Paul would see this through to the end, wherever the path might lead.

In the dense cover of jungle and night, Paul quietly moved among the trees, his mind plotting his next strategic moves. The mayor's threats made one thing clear, it was time to take the fight to the enemy's doorstep. He spent the coming days gathering intelligence through increasingly brazen acts of sabotage and surveillance.

He and Mackenzie had infiltrated the mayor's compound under darkness, planting covert listening devices and obtaining damning records from the man's private files.

Breaking into the mayor's house had been a test of wits and nerves. Mackenzie and Paul carefully bypassed the alarm system, slipping inside like shadows in the night. Paul took care of the listening devices, planting them strategically to catch any whispers of deceit. Mackenzie played lookout, her instincts sharp as ever. It was a risky move, but in this game of shadows, sometimes you must risk all to unveil the truth.

It was a delicate dance between planting seeds of doubt and ensuring their sources remained untraceable. Mackenzie was insistent on crafting a narrative that would stir up just enough controversy without revealing their true intentions. They debated the timing, the choice of words, and the potential repercussions. It was a chess game, each move calculated to unsettle those in power without causing a full-blown upheaval.

Paul seeded rumors and misinformation among the mayor's allies, slowly turning them against one another as paranoia took root, the power of whispers and half-truths. He strategically leaked information about the mayor's shady dealings to local reporters and trusted individuals. He shed light on the mayor's clandestine meetings and hinted at a darker underbelly to his seemingly innocent facade.

The rumor mill spun tales of the mayor's corruption and deceit, casting a shadow over his once-untarnished reputation. Sometimes, Paul reasoned, a well-placed seed of doubt can sow chaos in even the most meticulously crafted façade. With each new discovery leaked anonymously online and passed among locals, the mayor's control began slipping as more and more grew aware of the man's true nature.

As suspicion and unrest simmered below the surface, Paul continued gathering ammunition to dismantle the empire of corruption piece by piece. Soon, the mayor would face a betrayal of his own and be exposed for all to see on the island's terms. Paul was determined to outmaneuver his powerful opponent at every turn until the battle was won. With his plan falling neatly into place, Paul stayed two steps ahead of the mayor's thugs. He would turn the tables and vanquish the shadows of corruption through guile where brute force could not. The game was afoot, and checkmate loomed ever closer.

As Paul's hits against the mayor intensified, so too did the man's wrath. Bolder acts of sabotage drew ever closer inspection from hostile eyes. Paul realized his days of operating in shadows alone were numbered unless the final blow could be struck.

He met with Mackenzie under the cover of the darkening night, revealing the extent of his findings and the endgame plan to dismantle the criminal enterprise for good. Though wary, Mackenzie agreed to aid one final operation that would either doom them or destroy their enemy.

As the night of reckoning approached. Paul and Mackenzie infiltrated city hall, planting a digital bomb to expose the mayor's misdeeds once and for all.

But as they escaped into the jungle, shouts rang out, they were no longer the hunters, but the hunted. Flashlights pierced the forest as pursuers closed in.

Flashlights pierced the forest as pursuers closed in. Paul and Mackenzie fled through the thick foliage, evading capture in mere moments. They parted ways with the understanding their fates were now inextricably sealed, succeed together, or fall together into the shadows dogging their every step.

CHAPTER SIX

In Too Deep

F LEEING TO THE ABANDONED SHACK, THEY HID IN A SMALL STOR-
AGE room in the rear of the shack.

"Someone's coming," Mackenzie whispered. The front door swung open, flooding the small space with light. Two hooded figures stood silhouetted, peering inside.

"I thought I heard noises," one said. "Check it out."

Mackenzie grabbed Paul's arm and pulled him toward the back. But there was no other way out. They were trapped as the men stepped closer, searching. By the light of a raised lantern, their hiding spot would soon be discovered. Mackenzie dragged Paul into the deepest shadow behind a stack of crates. They held their breath as booted feet walked past.

One of the men grunted. "Nothing here." The lantern light moved toward the door, giving Paul and Mackenzie hope for escape. But then another set of footsteps sounded outside, followed by deep voices.

"Hey boys, they ain't getting far. Spread out and check the perimeter."

Mackenzie cursed under her breath. They were trapped with no way out. If they tried to sneak past now, the open door would frame them in silhouetted light. Paul squeezed her arm twice, the signal they'd devised for danger. Staying low, they exited the storage room and crept along the wall toward the front. A sliver of darkness remained between waiting men. If they could just slip by unnoticed...

But as Mackenzie peered around the crates, her foot scuffed the floor. Two sets of eyes snapped in their direction. They'd been spotted!

The armed men advanced with pistols raised. Paul stepped forward, palms up, blocking Mackenzie.

"Don't shoot," he said calmly. "We just got lost in the dark."

"What're you doin' sneakin' around here?" one growled.

"We heard noises and got curious." Paul kept his voice level. "No harm done."

"You have been snoopin' where you don't belong." Probably just a couple of rats," the other sneered. "But the boss doesn't like trespassers."

"Please, we'll leave peacefully." Paul fought to keep eye contact, standing his ground.

The men exchanged a glance. Finally, one jabbed his pistol at Paul. "Consider this a warning. Next time we find you here, we shoot first and ask questions later. Now get!"

Paul nodded respectfully and backed away, guiding a tense Mackenzie with him. They managed to slip past without a violent incident, but the threats lingered heavily in the quiet night. Trouble was coming, and fast. They had struck too close to the heart of this place. Paul and Mackenzie hurried into the cover of towering jungle ferns.

But before they'd gone far, shouts rose from the shed alongside the cracking of guns.

"Run!" Paul pushed Mackenzie ahead of him through the maze of foliage. Bullets whined past as they darted between the thick tree trunks. Their pursuers crashed through the brush, closing in. Paul risked a glance back, he could just make out dark silhouettes weaving after them. If those men caught up...

A shot ricocheted off a tree near Mackenzie's head. She dropped and rolled, coming up with her pistol drawn. Paul pulled her urgently along as their return fire echoed through the trees. There was no losing their hunters in the dense growth. Their only hope lay in outrunning the gunmen long enough to shake them at the tree line. Muscles burning, they plunged on into the sheltering night, bullets whining all around as the men gave chase through the shadowy jungle.

As the dense jungle enveloped them, its canopy whispering secrets of times long past, Mackenzie and Paul became shadows in the night. The faint moonlight glinted off the foliage, guiding their desperate flight as they evaded the pursuers. Paul's senses, honed by years of chasing shadows, warned him of every footfall, every rustle that betrayed the hunters' presence. It was a game of patience and skill, navigating the tangled paths known only to those attuned to the island's heartbeat.

They moved as one, a dance of survival in the face of unseen danger. And then, a change in the night's melody signaled their relief. The echoes of pursuit faded into the silence of the jungle, swallowed by the darkness. Paul felt it in the air, that shift when danger retreats and the hunted become the hunters. Mackenzie's eyes met Paul's, mirroring the silent understanding that they had eluded their foes through cunning and sheer will.

In that moment of stillness, amid the towering trees and the symphony of nocturnal creatures, Paul knew they had escaped the clutches of those who sought to silence them. But the jungle, unforgiving and relentless, reminded him that their rest was fleeting. For the hunt was far from over, and the shadows held darker secrets yet to be revealed.

After leaving their pursuers behind in the dense undergrowth, Paul and Mackenzie collapsed, spent, and scared, under the cover of thick branches.

"Paul, what now?" Mackenzie panted, leaning on her knees. "We're lost in the dark." He listened intently, hearing only the rustle of night creatures in the surrounding trees. Their stalkers seemed to have given up the chase for now.

"We find shelter till dawn, then get our bearings," he whispered. "This way, stick close to the trees. Paul guided them deeper into the ancient forest, keeping one arm on a moss-covered tree to orient them. Thanks to his years in service, he knew how to make the most of limited resources.

Up ahead, Paul spotted a small stone outcropping overgrown with vines. Just big enough to squeeze into and get out of the night air.

"Come on, almost there." Soon, they were curled up under nature's protection, catching their breath as the adrenaline wore off. Morning would bring new dangers, but for now, they were safe, and Paul's skills had seen them through another trial in the jungle's depths.

"Rest now, I'll keep watch," he urged Mackenzie.

When daylight's first glow filtered through the vines, Paul woke Mackenzie gently. She stirred with a wan smile of thanks as he offered her a drink from his flask.

"Time to move," he said. "Can you walk?" Mackenzie nodded, stretching tired legs. They peered cautiously out, relieved by the beauty of a new tropical dawn. But danger still lurked beneath the surface.

"I don't think they followed us," Paul surmised. "But it's not safe here either. Which way to the coast?"

She pointed southeast, then hesitated. "Paul...what if they come after my family? I can't put them at risk."

He grasped her shoulder. "We'll protect each other. And once the truth is out, these people will have no power left. Come on, one step at a time."

Mackenzie took a breath and fell in behind Paul's steady footsteps, leaving the shadows of the night behind. But she feared the future, while he burned more fiercely with the need to see justice done for Jane and all the rest. Their fight was just beginning.

As the sun rose higher, Paul and Mackenzie trekked through the jungle, hoping to circle around Cole's property unseen. But after their close call, they knew their faces were now known to the enemy.

"We're not getting out of this quietly, are we?" Mackenzie sighed. "They'll be hunting us."

Paul nodded grimly. "We've seen too much and asked the wrong questions. But now the whole island will hear the truth. No more disappearing dissenters in the night."

Mackenzie checked her weapon, her brow creased. "It's one thing to snoop around. Another is to have targets on our backs. How do we expose corruption when just staying alive each day is a battle?"

"A good question." Paul surveyed the jungle, formulating a plan. "For now, we need supplies and weapons. Then it's time those in power realized, that covering up their crimes just makes the people more determined to see justice done. No matter the cost, the truth will come out."

After a perilous trek through the jungle, Paul and Mackenzie finally emerged onto a familiar stretch of coastal road. The trees gave way to market stalls and weathered buildings in the poor village district. People glanced up warily at their ragged appearance, then hurried past with lowered eyes. Paul doubted anyone would aid them now. Not with Cole's men surely watching for any sign of the fugitives.

"We lay low and restock, then slip out of town after dark," Paul murmured.

"Best not linger where they expect to find us." Mackenzie nodded, hand lingering near her pistol. "I never thought it would come to this. Having to watch every shadow like the enemy is just around the corner."

"They are the enemy now." Paul scanned the alleys as they strode between stalls, feeling knives almost physically at their backs. But he told himself, "Let them come. I'm not running anymore. It's time this place knew what corruption has cost." With that thought burning as fierce as the tropical sun, Paul led the way deeper into the harbor of danger. Ready now to face whatever storms awaited them.

The walls were closing in from all sides, danger rising to new heights. Soon, the island would witness the fruits of his crusade, or his efforts would end in ruin and blood. Only time would tell what shadows might emerge victorious from the brewing maelstrom.

CHAPTER SEVEN

Friends and Foes

WITH LAST NIGHT'S INCIDENT BURNING BRIGHTLY IN HIS MIND, Paul gazed out from his front porch at the darkening jungle as the rains began to fall. Heavy droplets drummed the dense canopy above, their rhythmic display a palpable reminder of the impending storm.

Soon after, headlights pierced the gloom, flashing twice in the agreed signal. Mackenzie emerged from her cruiser, dashing through the downpour with an oilskin-wrapped bundle in her arms.

"It's all here," she said, unfolding the tarp to reveal files sodden with rain. Working together by lantern light, they spread the documents across a rough-hewn table. Paul examined the topmost paper with care, tracing faded words with a callused fingertip.

Mackenzie had sourced the files from a confidential informant who had finally decided to share some valuable information with her. The details in those files shed light on a longstanding mystery surrounding a series of unsolved crimes in the city. Mackenzie's timely intervention certainly pushed the investigation on the island of St. Anne. The importance of those files cannot be overstated; they were the missing pieces of the puzzle Paul had been striving to solve.

"Look at this permit," he said slowly. "It allows waste to be dumped in the same river everyone draws their water from. The chemicals alone could poison the whole island."

Mackenzie inhaled sharply. "I've had my suspicions, but proof like this..."

Her voice trailed off as she shuffled through more sheets. Gas receipts, payroll records, diagrams of tunnels leading from the mayor's compound, the corruption seemed to have no bottom. A long silence stretched between them as the import of these finds sank in.

At last, Mackenzie looked up, resolved to harden her features. "You were right to push this case. With evidence stacking up, we have to see it through to the end, wherever that leads." Her eyes held Paul's steady gaze. "I'm with you, especially after last night, for justice and this place we both still call home." Her oath eased some small part of Paul's burden. But as thunder rumbled in the east, he knew the dark days had only just begun.

"Mackenzie, before you leave, I want to thank you for these files. You know how valuable they are to our case," Paul said, studying the documents intently.

She smiled softly, her eyes reflecting a mix of relief and determination. "I'm glad I could help, Paul. I believe we're one step closer to uncovering the truth behind all this."

He nodded in agreement. "There's no doubt about that. Your efforts have not gone unnoticed. Stay safe on your way home, and let's reconvene soon to discuss our next move."

With a nod of understanding, Mackenzie gathered her belongings and headed towards the door. "Be careful, Paul. We'll catch up soon."

And with that, she left, leaving Paul to delve deeper into the secrets those files held.

Mackenzie drove home in the downpour, exhausted. She tried to get some sleep, but tossed restlessly into the small hours, shadows playing upon her walls. When exhaustion finally took her, her dreams were troubled, shapeless threats lurking at the tree line, a dark form looming over her prone body.

She awoke with a start to unfamiliar sounds outside. Fumbling for her sidearm, Mackenzie crept from her bed on silent feet, every sense straining against the pre-dawn gloom. The noises turned into something mundane, rodents rummaging for scraps of food. But her pulse still raced as a lone owl hooted mockingly from the treetops.

Later that morning, after a shower and several cups of coffee, she met Paul at their rendezvous spot by a sluggish stream. Mackenzie's unease showed plainly.

"Paul, we're in this deeper than I planned," she confessed in an undertone. "My superiors have made it clear to me, drop this case or suffer the consequences."

Her eyes, shadowed and fearful, pleaded for him to understand. "This corruption, it's like a hydra, cut off one head and two more take its place. Going against them alone, I'm as good as dead. So, what do we do, keep pushing, and hope justice is served before they turn on us in earnest?"

Paul listened without reply, weighing their dwindling options. His resolve had only hardened, but now another's safety rode on seeing this through.

His thoughts wandered back to Zoe Walker, a former detective here on the island. He worked with Zoe on a tough case that went back years before his retirement. He can't afford to live through that again. Mackenzie watched turmoil war across Paul's weathered features.

"I won't ask you to continue risking your life," he said at last. "This corruption, it's mine to see dismantled now."

But she shook her head vehemently. "Don't cut me out, not after we've come this far. These people need someone in Blue to have their backs." Her eyes held his, pleading. "And you'll never root it all out alone. Let me stand with you a while longer."

Paul sighed, knowing the justice she fought for, the island they both loved, these were worth any cost. And together, their chances improved. Still, the threats closed in like jaws from every side.

"The danger's grave, as you well know. But I promise this, no harm will come to you while there's life in my body." His promise rang with steel. Mackenzie dared to embrace him, taking comfort in sheltering arms.

"Then on we go," she said, strengthening her own resolve. Dark days lay ahead, but together they would weather the storm. Duty and friendship bound them now in the coming battle to rip corruption from these shores.

Paul and Mackenzie waited near the stream in silence as midnight came and went. Underbrush whispered and insect songs wove the jungle's nocturne, but no other sounds disturbed the darkness enclosing their hide.

Then, a subtle snap of twigs. Headlights winked through the foliage, advancing ponderously up the rutted track. Paul raised night-vision goggles and peered intently at the vehicle laboring into view, a rusted pickup truck, bulging with indistinct cargo. Two hooded figures rode inside, muttering and passing a bottle between them.

As it backfired past, Paul caught a glimpse of familiar features, Delgado, a known enforcer who frequented the wrong side of the mayor's dealings. He's known for his shady dealings and connections to unsavory characters. Delgado is a burly man with a scar running down his left cheek. As for his police record, it's as colorful as his reputation. Delgado isn't one to shy away from trouble,

Exchanging nods, he and Mackenzie melted from their hiding place into the truck's boiling wake. They tracked the growling engine off-road, picking their way barefoot down a muddy trail. The truck grumbled to a halt outside a ramshackle compound, dim lights bleeding through chinks in weathered walls. Voices carried on a breeze as figures passed in and out of the feeble glow.

Mackenzie nudged Paul and nodded toward a half-seen exchange, cash, and bundled packages trading hands. Her meaning was clear, with patience and stealth, their noose might tighten on these lawless outskirts. But greater dangers surely lurked within that den of thieves. Delgado set off alone along a twisting game trail, lost in muzzy thought. Paul signaled and together he and Mackenzie followed, moving soundless as darkness through the sweating jungle. Their quarry's erratic course wound ever deeper into the interior, where primal densities swallowed the last glow from distant camps. Roots grabbed at their bare feet; the canopy writhed like living curtains overhead. Delgado neither slowed nor looked back, trusting trees and night to shield his solitude.

At last, he emerged into a small clearing. Here he stopped short, cocking his head as if listening for pursuers. But the jungle held its breath, and some minutes passed before he relaxed and crouched by a massive tree's gnarled base. Patting moss-slick bark, Delgado loosened a hidden hatch and rummaged within, withdrawing a leather pouch. From this he counted bills by the glow of the moon, slipping a few into his pocket before locking it up once more.

Paul and Mackenzie, nearly blending with the surrounding dark, observed in cautious silence. Only when their quarry had vanished once more did they inch forward, laying hands upon the tree's secrets, and finding, to their fast-beating hearts, the first sure signs that justice might at long last be near.

Delgado did not notice the shadows following his footsteps as he plunged once more into the forested night. Paul gestured for Mackenzie to remain hidden while he followed closer, letting instinct guide his movements. The trees spoke amongst themselves as man and shadow traveled their separate paths. Paul glimpsed shattered moonlight flickering in Delgado's motion, keeping pace just beyond sight. His senses tingled, something more awaited here if only he could stay close enough to find it.

Finally, Delgado paused again, booted toe scuffing at a trampled patch of earth and exhaling sharply through clenched teeth. Paul crouched behind screening leaves and saw, with a detective's eye, what the criminal's impatience nearly missed, a spot where soil had been dug and replaced in haste, lacking the jungle's unblemished randomness.

Delgado cursed and spat, kicking harder at the patch before

stalking off in foul temper. Only then did Paul emerge, falling to his knees and gently scraping away the disturbed layer. His fingers closed around cold metal, a key, it's cut unmarred by time, promising untold secrets to be unearthed in the twilight where wrongs were beginning to rise.

Some time had passed exploring the clearing where Paul unearthed the tarnished key. Together, Paul and Mackenzie searched diligently until unearthing a locked metal grate, which concealed further clues. Now, with renewed vigor, their minds turned to piecing together each fragment of the dark tapestry weaving around them.

Mackenzie turned to Paul, "With Delgado and these others using the woods for their hidden stashes, who knows what else we may discover out here? The trail could stretch far."

Paul nodded slowly. "But the next step is clear. At first light, we will return to search where that ground was disturbed. Whatever lies beneath may offer answers and ways to apply new pressures."

His eyes met hers with determination. A plan was forming, risky but with justice as their plumb line. Come tomorrow, they would continue pushing back the shadows, following each lead into the thickening mist wherever it may take them.

The rain eased as darkness deepened around their remote camp. Between sips of coffee, Paul and Mackenzie spoke in low voices of allies and enemies, plans laid, and hints unearthed, tightening the net around corruption inch by inch. Their bond had strengthened through shared purpose, but also in unspoken ways neither dared name just yet. In each other, they found refuge from the storm without and within, two souls standing fast against the shadows lengthening across this land.

Mackenzie smiled sadly. "Who'd have thought that we'd get this far? But the closer we get to the truth, the harder they'll fight to bury it again." Her eyes seemed to gauge how close that fight had drawn.

Paul gazed into the jungle. By sunrise the die could be cast, their choices narrow to stand together at the brink or face what came alone. Whichever path they trod, one thing was sworn, these shores would know justice's hand before their crusade ended. With that unspoken vow, they lay down to rest under canvas, whispering in the deep. Come dawn, their bond would be tested as the noose drew taut around the trails they now must follow to the ends of justice or themselves.

CHAPTER EIGHT

Into the Lion's Den

IN THE PREDAWN LIGHT, PAUL AND MACKENZIE COVERTLY NAVI-GATED their way through the dense jungle foliage toward Evan Cole's remote property. The moonlight filtering through the tree canopy provided little illumination, forcing them to rely heavily on their senses as they carefully picked their way over twisted roots and squeezed between towering trunks.

Up ahead, they spotted the first signs of civilization, a dilapidated fence coming into view, its rusted barbed wire angling off into the shadows. Moving with calm precision, they skirted the perimeter until Paul spotted a breach in the wood slats. He signaled to Mackenzie, and they paused, listening intently for any sounds of activity on the other side. Only the drone of insects and an occasional hooting owl responded.

Satisfied the coast was clear, they slipped through the opening one at a time. Before them lay a landscape of ramshackle sheds and an aging main house in varying states of disrepair. A few solitary lights shone dimly from within but revealed no signs of movement. Paul motioned for Mackenzie to follow as they launched their clandestine investigation, gliding like ghosts between the shadows.

It was like treading on thin ice, every step they took was calculated and cautious. Mackenzie, always quick on her feet, whispered, "Paul, watch out for that loose branch on the right."

Paul replied in a low tone, "Thanks. Keep an eye on the back entrance; we can't afford any slip-ups."

The air was thick with tension, but they moved with synchronicity, each step bringing them closer to the truth they sought. It was moments like those that tested their resolve and showcased their unbreakable bond in the pursuit of justice.

Their senses were on high alert; they surveyed the grounds for clues. But what mysteries and dangers awaited them within Cole's isolated domain under cover of this inky tropical night? Utilizing tracking skills honed from years of fieldwork, Paul and Mackenzie swept their surroundings, picking up subtle signs that warned of potential threats. As they crept along the edge of the property, Paul halted abruptly and signaled for silence.

Through the dense foliage, they spotted the faint glow of cigarettes emerging from the tree line some distance ahead. Two silhouettes paced back and forth in overlapping routes of the guard, the crunch of boots through the undergrowth carrying clearly on the still night air.

Crouching low, Paul and Mackenzie studied the sentries' patterns, timing the gaps between passes. When both guards' backs were turned, they dashed soundlessly forward, flitting from tree to tree. As they hugged close to the gnarled trunks, the acrid scent of tobacco smoke drifted over on the breeze. Harsh, low voices carried an unintelligible mumble.

A twig snapped in the distance, drawing the guards' attention momentarily before they resumed their patrol. Paul and Mackenzie exhaled quiet breaths of relief before pressing on into deeper shadows. Whatever illicit activities transpired under Cole's watch, security was tight. Discovery could spell grave danger for their risky infiltration. Crouching low in the bushes, they observed the guards from a distance until an opportunity arose. When both men gazed out into the tree line, they darted between the intervals of sheds towards a large, ramshackle structure up ahead.

Reaching its worn walls, they began inspecting for clues. Paul ran his hands along the rough wood, noticing recent scrapes and gouges in the aging material. Kneeling, he lifted a handful of damp soil, allowing the fine grains to slip through his fingers. Among the dirt were bits of plaster and glass, evidence of demolition.

Motioning Mackenzie over, they peered around the building's perimeter and spotted a sizable depression in the ground a short distance away, along with scrap lumber and debris piled to one side. The unmistakable scent of dried paint hung faintly in the air.

It was clear someone had gone to great lengths to erase what once stood here. But to what end? What secrets were they desperate to conceal beneath the wet earth? Mackenzie met Paul's eyes, and in the darkness, a question lingered unspoken: had they at last stumbled upon the final resting place of those who dared cross Evan Cole?

A snapped branch in the woods sent them diving for cover once more. Their discovery would have to wait as more pressing dangers threatened exposure. Crouched low in the bushes, Paul scanned their surroundings with keen scrutiny. His tracking skills proved their worth once more as his gaze fell upon a patch of foliage that, upon closer inspection, appeared out of place. Signaling to Mackenzie, they carefully pulled back the dense vegetation to discover an old wooden hatch partially concealed beneath. Moss and mold grew thick across its surface, clinging stubbornly to rotting wood.

But telltale scrapes in the dirt around its edges revealed recent activity. Paul tested the hatch's grip, finding it unlocked. Exchanging a meaningful glance with Mackenzie, he lifted it open with utmost care to avoid any creaks or groans. Black emptiness yawned below, the dank scent of moist earth wafting up. Reaching into his pack, Paul retrieved a heavy-duty flashlight and flicked it on, angling the beam cautiously downward.

A narrow stone stairway led into unknown depths. Whatever kept company with the shadows down there was not meant for innocent eyes. Mackenzie readied her own light as Paul began a cautious descent, every sense alert for impending danger. They had finally located a hidden entry point that may yet yield the dark secrets eluding them thus far.

Mackenzie, cautious as ever hesitated, showed a flicker of uncertainty in her eyes. The unknown can be unsettling, but her resolve matched Paul's as they stepped into the murky depths, ready to face whatever lay ahead. Paul descended the stairs with deliberate care, testing each step before placing his full weight as Mackenzie followed close behind. At the bottom, their flashlight beams cut swaths through the engulfing black, illuminating a low stone chamber. Cobwebs clung thickly to the ceiling corners, and a faint, musty smell hung on the stale air. Papers, file folders, and loose photos were strewn across a worn table as if rifled through in haste.

Stepping further into the gloomy space, Paul and Mackenzie aimed their flashlights across the documents, hearts pounding in a silence broken only by their own quiet breaths. What they found gave them cause for grave concern. Spread before them were financial records detailing offshore transactions, photos of meetings with known criminals and associates of the mayor, catalogs of smuggled goods, and damning letters arranging drops and payoffs. It was evident from the discarded mess that Cole was a lynchpin in the corrupt network, weaving its insidious influence across the entire island.

Stifling gasps, Paul and Mackenzie exchanged stern looks by flashlight. They had uncovered the strongest proof yet of a criminal operation that went far deeper than they'd imagined, with roots running directly into city hall. But further mysteries beckoned in the dark recesses as they swept their beams around the room, uncovering secrets no one was meant to find.

Paul and Mackenzie froze, exchanging a panicked glance as footsteps crunched audibly across the ground above. Their lights extinguished in an instant as they fused into the shadows, scarcely daring to breathe. Muffled voices drifted down, words unclear but tones concerned. Footsteps rustling, voices whispering, and orders barked as a clearly agitated search ensued. Harsh orders growled for the grounds to be combed. The hunt was on.

Heartbeats thundered in Paul and Mackenzie's ears as they willed themselves unseen. They dare not utter a single word.

A creak on the stairs caused them to flatten further against the damp stone wall, every instinct screaming to flee, yet their feet were locked in place. Heavy boots descended slowly, the intruder's flashlight beam stretching out before him. As the yellow shaft swept across their hiding spot, Paul reacted with fluid precision.

Emerging from the dark like a vengeful spirit, he rammed the back of his light into the man's jaw with a sickening crack before bear-hugging him into motionless silence.

Mackenzie seized the fallen light as more footsteps approached, poised to engage. They had moments before discovery, and evading capture in these close quarters promised a battle. With fateful choices looming in the flashlight's glow, could they escape the net closing tight around them, or would the hunters' blood be spilled this night?

Paul grabbed Mackenzie's wrist, and they lunged into the stairwell and furiously climbed upwards. Gunfire erupted as their pursuers spotted movement, ricochets hammering off the stone with lethal speed. Bursting into the tropical night, they plunged at a dead sprint into the merciless jungle. Flashlights and shouts closed in from behind as an entire compound gave chase. Paul peeled left, dragging Mackenzie into a harried dash between tight tree trunks.

Branches lashed their flesh, and twisted roots sought to trip them in the darkness. Mackenzie fought to keep pace through the churning undergrowth as orange muzzle flashes lit the canopy. Bullets whizzed past with dangerous accuracy. Their pursuers were skilled trackers pressing the hunt. As the terrain grew steeper, Paul swung onto a narrow game trail up the slope. Pebbles scattered and crunched deafeningly underfoot. Thorns tore at clothing and skin alike, yet they pushed on, driven by survival instinct alone. Somewhere below, dogs joined the mayhem with snarls and barks.

Lungs burning, muscles screaming, they crested the ridge just as pale dawn light breached the east. Behind stretched a snaking ribbon of trampled forest, their scent trail fresh for trackers on the warpath.

Paul and Mackenzie flew down the steep slopes, the sounds of pursuit relentless through the moonlit jungle. Their adrenaline masked exhaustion as sharp branches clawed at their clothing. A howl rose from the darkness, answered by others; the hunting pack had found their trail. Eyes gleamed between the trees as more joined the coordinated drive. Paul spurred Mackenzie faster, determined to outrun teeth and triggers alike.

They splashed across a shallow stream, hoping the moving water hid their scent. But the barking grew nearer, encouraged by another flanking maneuver. Up ahead, tree roots had undermined the bank; a simple drop awaited one misstep. Paul maneuvered surefooted as Mackenzie scrambled after, their fleeting footfalls echoed by thundering paws.

A shot rang out from the opposite direction!

From seemingly nowhere, aid came, startling birds from the canopy in riotous wings. Paul smiled, recognizing an old friend's call. Hidden eyes observed the chase. A distraction arose and the pack wavered, confusion slowing their bloodlust. Mackenzie found new strength, racing on instinct beside the river now shining with predators' reflections.

Their unexpected aid came in the form of an enigmatic ally named Diego. A mysterious figure with his own agenda, yet aligned with Paul's mission to uncover the truth. Diego's arrival turned the tide in Paul and Mackenzie's favor, shedding light on the darkness that threatened to consume them.

Diego appeared like a guardian angel, his presence a beacon of hope in the darkness. With swift action, he skillfully disarmed their pursuers, his movements calculated and precise. "You two alright?" he asked, his voice steady and reassuring.

Diego led Paul and Mackenzie through the dense forest, and his knowledge of the terrain was evident in every step he took. The path to a hidden cabin was a labyrinth of twisted roots and overgrown foliage, yet Diego navigated it with ease, guiding them like a true protector. Along the way, he shared bits of wisdom and stories of survival, his words a comforting soundtrack to our journey through the unknown.

And as mysteriously as Diego appeared, he disappeared into the jungle without a word spoken.

Their safehouse appeared through the trees as if salvation's light was a beacon in the dark. They dashed through the curtain of vines, collapsing within laughing despite hell nipping at their heels. Safe, for now, in the tropical night's dying folds.

CHAPTER NINE

Following the Money Trail

MACKENZIE AND PAUL WERE HOLED UP IN A SAFE HOUSE ON THE outskirts of town. It was a weather-beaten cottage, its paint peeling under the relentless sun, nestled in a dense thicket of palm trees and bougainvillea. It was almost completely camouflaged by the lush greenery that shielded it from prying eyes.

The owner of the 'safehouse" is a reclusive old fisherman by the name of Elias, a friend of Diego, who had his reasons for keeping it off the grid.

The structure itself was sturdy, with reinforced doors and windows that could withstand a storm. Elias had equipped it with basic supplies such as canned goods, water purifiers, and a shortwave radio for emergencies. But what truly made it secure was its location, hidden in plain sight yet invisible to those who weren't looking for it. It provided Paul and Mackenzie a sanctuary to strategize, analyze evidence, and plan their next move without the shadow of the corrupt forces looming over them.

After catching their breath and rehydrating, Paul and Mackenzie dumped all the evidence they had gathered onto a small table. They sorted through the piles of damp documents by candlelight in the cramped safehouse.

"Look at this," said Mackenzie, passing Paul a ledger. Dates and figures were meticulously recorded, documenting massive cash transactions laundered through Cole's logging business. Names of political donors and known criminals dotted the pages. Paul examined the names.

"These donations lined the pockets of everyone with power on the island. No wonder Cole and the mayor are untouchable."

Flipping through photographs, Mackenzie gasped. "Paul, these were taken at Johnny's Bar. I recognize the men from my patrols." She showed Paul pictures of suspicious exchanges, the mayor grinning alongside gunrunners. Corruption is rooted deeply in every branch of power.

"With this, we can prove a public money laundering ring reaches the highest levels," Paul said. "But it still doesn't tell us Jane's story. There's more to uncover."

Paul pieced together his suspicions. "Jane was helping villagers in debt to Cole. I'll wager she found these documents by accident, and then she posed too great a threat to those involved."

A theory emerged Paul believed was worth pursuing. He and Mackenzie now hold smoking guns to expose corruption if they can evade those determined to bury the truth forever. Paul noticed one file was labeled with a woman's name. Inside were bank statements and records of mortgages. Scanning the pages, Paul's eyes grew wide.

"Mackenzie, look at this. Jane wasn't a charity worker; she was a bank manager." Mackenzie took the file. "The Community Bank of St. Anne. So that's how she discovered the money laundering."

Paul continued, "Cole and the mayor used her bank to clean dirty funds. But Jane found inconsistencies in the accounts. See here; she noted discrepancies between official reports and actual transactions."

"She must have confronted Cole," Mackenzie guessed. "He couldn't risk her going to authorities."

A new picture emerged of Jane as a brave woman fighting corruption from within the system. Paul said, "This gives her kidnapping true motive. Cole and the mayor tried to silence her to keep their crimes hidden."

Mackenzie shook her head. "All this time, we thought she worked with a charity. But she was an undercover warrior for justice, in her own way."

"Now we know why they took her," Paul said. "And we have the proof to make them answer for it."

Within the files, Paul discovered Jane's handwritten notes. He read her familiar script under the candle's warm glow. Jane questioned everything as discrepancies arose. She wrote of threats from Cole as her discoveries pointed to him. "If I expose this, they will harm me and the villagers. But I must find the truth."

Her journal told of her late nights reviewing records, seeking any clues. Jane wrote, "Everyone says it's best not to cross Cole, but the bank is being used for illegal schemes. I won't be silent while they exploit our people. They will stop at nothing to cover this up. I've arranged files in a safe place if anything happens to me." Paul realized those files must have been what led him and Mackenzie to the clearing in the jungle.

Jane's last entry chilled him. "I've set up a meeting with the authorities. With any luck, this will be exposed, and I can protect the others. If not, may justice find its own way." Brave Jane had walked with her eyes open into the storm, hoping to shield the villagers from its wrath. Now, her fate was seared into Paul's memory, fueling his fire to see her vision of justice fulfilled. Paul studied the clues before him, Jane's meticulous documentation, and her determined final entries. Slowly, an understanding took shape.

"She wasn't kidnapped for what she knew," Paul said slowly. "It was for what she threatened to do with that knowledge."

Mackenzie looked up. "Exposing the corruption network."

Paul nodded. "Cole and the mayor couldn't risk Jane meeting with officials. Not when she had evidence that could topple their entire operation."

"So, they tried to silence her before she could blow the whistle," Mackenzie said grimly.

A stirring mix of grief and outrage filled Paul. Jane had almost given her life in pursuit of a just world, only to be struck down on the cusp of success.

"We have to keep her promise," he said.

Mackenzie met his gaze and nodded. "Have you spoken to Jane since she left the clinic?" Jane asked.

"Not since I snuck her out of the clinic and put her on a boat to Guadeloupe."

Paul contacted his friend Detective Zoe Walker on the nearby island of Guadeloupe and asked her to hide Jane somewhere on the island until this case was solved. Jane was staying in a safe house in Deshaies under an assumed name.

United in their purpose, Paul and Mackenzie resumed sorting documents by candlelight. With each new revelation, their conviction grew stronger. Jane had shown immense courage; now it was time for Paul and Mackenzie to follow her brave example and shine a light on the shadows haunting St. Anne's shores. Paul ran a hand over his tired face. The weight of their discoveries dragged at his spirit.

Mackenzie noticed. "What is it?"

"Jane was taken for her integrity," Paul replied grimly. "Cole and the mayor have shown they'll try to kill, and have killed, to cover their crimes." He turned to her. "We're wading into deep waters, up against ruthless men who'll stop at nothing. There may be no way back from this."

Mackenzie nodded slowly. "I knew the risks when we started. But this corruption runs too deep to stop now; we have to see this through."

Paul admired her courage, though concern gripped him. "Once we expose them, we'll have crossed a line. They won't let us live as witnesses."

"Then we'll have to stay one step ahead," she said firmly.

Her determination heartened Paul. Still, as the candles flickered against the night, he could not escape the shadows of what lay ahead. Their enemies held all the power unless they could outsmart them at their own game.

Paul gazed into the candle flames, processing it all. "Jane was silenced to protect more than money laundering," he said. Mackenzie looked up questioningly.

"Follow me. Jane finds corruption at the bank. That corruption funds shady political operations, buying influence far beyond this island. If word got out..."

"It could topple more than the mayor," Mackenzie breathed, understanding. "These people have connections with power we can't imagine."

Paul nodded grimly. "Destroying Jane's evidence and threatening the living was about self-preservation on a massive scale. When justice is a liability, you remove it by any means."

His eyes hardened with determination. "But it also gives us leverage. Once we distribute proof of their plots, from the bank to the backroom deals, no corner of their empire will be safe from the truth."

Mackenzie felt her own fire renewed. "With their operations exposed, they'll have no choice left but to run from the law. And we'll be there to make sure they never find a safe harbor again."

Their mission had grown larger than the island but also more pivotal. They now had to fight for every soul oppressed under the shadow of corruption. Paul rubbed his tired eyes as daylight filtered through cracks in the hut. Their discovery filled him with purpose but also exhaustion.

Mackenzie saw his weariness. "We've come too far to let fatigue cloud our judgment. We need proof that will stand up in court."

Paul nodded. "Once we start exposing this, there's no turning back. We have to make sure our case is airtight." They poured over documents again, organizing a digital archive of the money trail, witness accounts, photos, and communications. All told the deeper story of how corruption festered.

Paul knew they had to secure the found documents securely and safely. With the stakes high and danger lurking, he needed to ensure that even if the physical evidence was compromised, the truth wouldn't be lost. Included with the other gear he packed in his backpack, he had brought along a portable scanner, a trusty companion in his investigative endeavors. Carefully scanning each page and preserving every detail, he created a comprehensive digital archive. These files were then encrypted and backed up on multiple secure drives hidden in various locations for safekeeping.

One such location was on the island of Guadeloupe with his former partner, Zoe Miller.

It was meticulous work but essential in safeguarding the evidence against any tampering or destructive attempts by the corrupt parties involved. Paul knew that in the world of crime-solving, creating a digital archive is akin to preserving the heart of a case, ensuring that no matter what transpires, the truth remains untarnished and ready to be revealed when the time is right.

"But we're missing the smoking gun that ties it definitively to Jane's kidnapping," Mackenzie said. Paul knew she was right. They had motives but no proof their enemies were physically involved. Not yet.

"We need to infiltrate their operations directly," he replied. "If we can plant recorders and cameras, perhaps we'll finally hear their confessions in their own words."

It was a dangerous plan, but one that could seal their enemies' fates for good. With renewed focus, Paul and Mackenzie began hatching their covert operation, preparing to strike at the heart of injustice on the island.

"We sneak in under cover of darkness," Paul explained. "Plant the devices where they're least likely to be found. Then we wait."

Mackenzie nodded slowly. It was a perilous plan, but Paul's strategic mind gave them an edge. "I'll follow your lead," she replied. "You've brought us this far."

Paul smiled tiredly. "I wouldn't have made it without your help. We're a team, for better or worse."

She placed a hand on his arm. "No matter the danger, I trust you with my life. And I vow to see this through to the end, by your side." Her words comforted Paul as night fell. Together, they'd confront terrors most ran from. But their bond was now unbreakable, forged in shared purpose against the darkness threatening to engulf the island.

Paul and Mackenzie, feeling it was now safe to leave their hiding place, went directly to an old, abandoned warehouse on the outskirts of town to keep an eye on the crooks. Leaving the safehouse was a tactical decision born out of necessity. The safehouse had served its purpose in safeguarding the critical evidence they had collected, but it was no longer the ideal location for their next move.

The abandoned warehouse was a good ten miles from downtown, tucked away in the neglected part of town where shadows seemed to linger longer than usual.

They walked about a mile through the dense jungle to a clearing just off an old logging road. There, stashed among the trees, was an old Chevy that belonged to a friend of Paul's, a car that's seen better days but still gets the job done. Mackenzie had thought they would have to walk the entire 10 miles. Paul never ceased to amaze her.

The location of the warehouse was like something out of a noir film: isolated and eerie. Graffiti covered the walls like a form of urban poetry, telling stories of those who passed through before them. As they approached the warehouse, a sense of foreboding crept up Paul's spine, a feeling that this was not going to be a simple walk in the park.

As they stashed the car about half a mile from the warehouse, they made the rest of the way on foot. In this line of work, problems are just part of the job. Whether it's a locked door, a hidden trap, or a lurking threat, one always finds a way to navigate through the darkness and uncover the truth.

The abandoned warehouse was shrouded in secrets and whispers of past illicit dealings that beckoned Paul. Its desolate walls and broken windows seemed to echo with the ghosts of the island's darker deeds. But beneath its neglected facade lay a treasure trove of clues waiting to be uncovered. They ventured to the warehouse seeking answers, knowing that certain associates of the mayor used it as a meeting place from time to time.

The significance of the warehouse lay in the secrets it held and the truths it promised to reveal. They needed to gather more evidence and understand their quarry's movements to piece together the puzzle they were facing. It was tense, but it was a necessary step in their investigation.

They approached the warehouse with caution, their senses honed and determination unyielding. Observing their enemies without drawing any attention to themselves required finesse and careful planning.

From the safety of shadows, Paul and Mackenzie watched their enemies conduct business as usual. But unknown to the corrupt, two sets of eyes were keenly documenting every transaction, call, and meeting, waiting to bring the whole rotten structure crashing down with a single exposure.

They positioned themselves strategically behind a nearby building, using binoculars to monitor movements. The cast of characters involved in this sinister play included known associates of the mayor and henchmen with a shady air and a readiness for violence. Their whispered conversations and exchanged glances hinted at a dangerous agenda lurking behind closed doors.

Paul had a small, discreet recorder with a sound microphone attached, capturing every word exchanged like a silent witness to their shady dealings. His focus was sharp, his senses keen as he picked up on the subtle nuances in their conversation, the hushed tones, the nervous glances, the careful choice of words.

As their conversation continued, Mackenzie scribbled down notes in her trusty old notebook, documenting every detail, every clue that would later prove to be crucial in unraveling the mayor's web of corruption. In this line of work, every word, every gesture, every fleeting expression held a key to unlocking the mystery at hand. And that day, they were one step closer to bringing justice to those who deserved it most.

Paul and Mackenzie continued to gather crucial information as the minutes ticked by: snippets of incriminating dialogue, transactions shrouded in secrecy, and hints of a larger web of corruption entangling the island. The conversation was nonexistent as Mackenzie continued to scribble down notes, her eyes sharp and focused, while Paul committed details to memory, piecing together the puzzle that lay before them. The tension in the air was unmistakable; every moment stretched taut with anticipation and danger.

They remained hidden for hours, tracking every move, until the early hours of dawn painted the sky in hues of gray. The darkness was their cloak, shielding them from detection as they unraveled the threads that bound their adversaries together in a sinister dance of deceit.

In the stillness of the night, secrets that were whispered on the wind found their mark in Paul's ears, guiding him one step closer to the heart of the corruption poisoning the once peaceful island.

Soon, the truth would be out, and justice would be done. They had come too far to stop now, with the fate of St. Anne's people hanging in the balance.

Chapter Ten

The Tangled Web Unwinds

PAUL TOOK A STEADYING BREATH AS HE PREPARED TO SET HIS PLAN in motion. For too long the people of St. Anne had lived under the shadow of corruption. Now, it was time to cast light on the truth.

He was tired of being in the jungle. He longed to see his beach, to hear the waves crashing against the shoreline.

After he and Mackenzie left their stakeout at the abandoned warehouse, they separated, each to their own isolated, safe place. Mackenzie went to a cousin's house on the other side of the island, desperate to get a shower and sleep.

Before venturing to the homes of friends and allies, Paul found himself strolling along the beach, the rhythmic sound of the waves a soothing backdrop to his contemplations. He knew he would be taking a chance. However, he had hoped his pursuers would not think Paul would be careless and return home.

But he knew it would have to be a quick visit.

In those solitary moments, with the salty breeze tangling his hair and the sand soft beneath his feet, Paul would reflect on the case at hand, turning over every detail in his mind like a well-worn puzzle waiting to be solved. The vast expanse of the ocean before him mirrored the endless possibilities and challenges that lay ahead, and in that solitude, he found clarity in the middle of the chaos.

Paul carried with him not just the weight of past experiences but also the unwavering determination to seek justice and bring light to the shadows that lurked in the corners of the world. The journey from contemplation to action was a familiar one, a path he had walked many times before, and each step brought him closer to unraveling the mysteries that awaited.

Using the dark of night as a cover, he slipped from his beachfront bungalow and reentered the jungle; he picked his way carefully, watching for those who sought him out. The moon provided just enough illumination to navigate without alerting any patrols. He remained vigilant for any signs of watchers along the route.

Finally reaching the outskirts of town, Paul cautiously made his way to the homes of those he had singled out as allies, friends, and reporters, people with integrity who could be trusted to spread the word without compromising his covert operation. One by one, he left packets containing the damning evidence on their doorsteps, along with cryptic notes to arrange secret meetings at dawn.

Paul's plan to expose the pervasive corruption on the island involved a strategic dissemination of incriminating information. He targeted select individuals embroiled in the mayor's web of deceit. These packets of information were like seeds of truth planted in the fertile soil of deception, destined to bloom into undeniable evidence.

Prominent figures such as Dr. Patel, the respected town physician, and Mrs. Jenkins, the owner of the local bookstore where Jane worked part-time, were recipients of these damning packets. Each of them represented a different facet of the island's community, from healers to educators, yet all were unwittingly entangled in the mayor's malevolent schemes.

By entrusting them with these revelations, Paul's aim was to rally allies against the tide of corruption and to kindle a flame of justice in the hearts of those who yearned for a brighter tomorrow. The recipients of these packets became silent partners in the battle for truth, their actions echoing across the island like a clarion call for change. In the face of darkness, these acts of courage and conviction illuminated a path toward a future where integrity and righteousness would reign once more on St. Anne's hallowed shores.

His final stop brought Paul to the home of a journalist, Kim

Wong, who had grown disillusioned with the mayor's tightening grip on the press. Kim Wong is a striking figure with ebony hair that falls in elegant waves and eyes that gleam with determination. Her presence commands attention, and her sharp features betray a keen intellect. But it is her unwavering quest for justice that defines her. Kim is like a beacon of truth in a world shrouded in darkness, fearless in her pursuit of exposing corruption and injustice. She stands as a testament to the power of a relentless spirit in the face of adversity.

Paul first met Kim Wong during a high-profile case back in his detective days. She was like a dog with a bone when it came to uncovering the truth, relentless in her pursuit of justice through her pen and paper. Their paths crossed when she was digging into a corruption scandal that led straight to the heart of the city's political elite. Kim's determination and sharp intellect impressed Paul, and he knew then that they shared a common goal: to shine a light on the darkness that others preferred to keep hidden.

Their interactions in the past were always professional yet tinged with mutual respect. Kim had a way of asking the tough questions, of probing deep into the heart of a story to reveal the bare facts beneath the layers of deceit. He admired her tenacity and her unwavering commitment to holding those in power accountable for their actions.

When Paul found himself standing at the doorstep of her home, it felt like a reunion of old allies, two individuals bound by a shared sense of duty and a desire to make a difference in a world where corruption and injustice often reigned supreme. He knew that together, they would uncover the truth that others were so desperate to keep buried, no matter the obstacles that stood in their way.

The exterior of Kim Wong's home reflected a blend of cultural influences, a harmonious fusion of traditional island architecture and modern sensibilities. Nestled amidst a grove of swaying coconut palms, the house stood as a testament to Kim's roots and her aspirations. The facade boasted intricate wooden carvings depicting scenes from local folklore and vibrant hues that glowed under the tropical sun. A tiled roof sloped gracefully, sheltering the veranda where potted orchids bloomed in riotous colors. The sound of wind chimes tinkling in the breeze added a melodic charm to the surroundings.

As Paul stood at the front door, his gaze taking in the ornate details and the subtle elegance of the home, he couldn't help but feel a sense of admiration for her aesthetic taste and cultural pride. It was a haven amid the turmoil that gripped the island, a sanctuary where tradition and modernity coexisted in perfect harmony.

In some ways, Kim Wong's home was what Paul expected. A home that exuded a warmth and authenticity that resonated with the image he had formed of her, a woman of strength, grace, and unwavering resolve. Yet, beneath the beauty of the exterior lay layers of complexity and intrigue, hinting at the secrets she harbored within those welcoming walls.

Paul tapped lightly to rouse her without disturbing the neighbors, then slipped the documents through the open mail slot on the front door with instructions to publish the revealing contents on her underground blog. Kim Wong is an intrepid journalist who fearlessly seeks the truth amidst the chaos. She is a sharp-witted and relentless reporter, unearthing hidden truths and shedding light on the shadows of corruption that plague St. Anne. She could play a crucial role in exposing the mayor's misdeeds, adding momentum to Paul's quest for justice. An invaluable ally in the fight against darkness.

With the first embers of scandal now lit, Paul retreated into the cover of night to watch his revelations begin to spread and consume the corruption that had poisoned the community for far too long. By daybreak, the fire would be well stoked and unstoppable. Justice was coming for the mayor and his corrupt regime.

Dawn's first light revealed signs that a storm was brewing. Word had quickly spread throughout St. Anne as residents huddled together to examine the documents Paul had leaked, gasping in horror at the depth of depravity that had poisoned their community.

In the town square, by noon, angry crowds swelled as the damning details of money laundering and Jane's kidnapping were shared from person to person. Chants of "Débusquer les corrupteurs!" grew louder, fueled by outrage against the injustice they had endured for too long. Kim's exposé post in her blog amplified the uproar, going viral as it was shared via screenshot repeatedly. She pulled no punches in laying full blame on the mayor and calling for public accountability.

At city hall, Mayor Harris tried desperately to downplay the allegations and dismiss them as political smears. But it was clear his authority was slipping as even loyal supporters distanced themselves from the toxicity. Demonstrators gathered outside the building, shouting for the mayor's resignation. Riot police were deployed to control the swelling protest, but many officers secretly sympathized with the movement. A general strike was called, shutting down businesses across the island as the populace united in demanding real change and prosecution of all involved in corruption.

The mayor released a response to the citizens of St. Anne, "As for those baseless accusations and calls for my resignation, let me assure you that I have weathered far worse storms in my time. The people of St. Anne know the truth about my intentions and the good work I do for this island."

Rumors and scandalous tales often swirl around those in positions of power, like me. It is regrettable that some individuals succumb to the temptation of spreading such falsehoods to undermine the stability and prosperity of our beloved island. Rest assured, I stand firm in my commitment to the welfare of St. Anne and its inhabitants."

The mayor's statement continued, "As for these baseless accusations, I can categorically proclaim that they are nothing more than fabrications concocted by those who seek to destabilize the peace we have worked tirelessly to maintain. My conscience is clear, and my hands are clean of any wrongdoing. I trust that the discerning residents of St. Anne will see through this smokescreen of deception and stand with me in upholding the integrity of our community.

In times of adversity, it is essential to stand steadfast and resolute in the face of adversity. The shadows of malice cast upon me shall dissipate like morning mist, revealing the truth and vindicating my unwavering dedication to the betterment of St. Anne."

Privately, the mayor admitted to his inner circle that a seed of doubt may have been planted in the minds of a few individuals due to the nature of these scandalous allegations. Saying, "I believe that the majority of the island's residents have unwavering faith in my integrity and leadership. They recognize the staunch commitment I have shown to our community over the years, steering us through both calm seas and tumultuous storms."

The words were falling on deaf ears.

He continued, "The bonds of trust I have nurtured with the people of St. Anne run deep, forged through years of dedicated service and genuine concern for their well-being. Despite the whispers of malice and the shadows of doubt cast upon me, my supporters stand resolute in their belief in my innocence and steadfast character. Indeed, the resilience and unity of our community in times of adversity serve as a testament to the enduring spirit of St. Anne. Rest assured, my friends, that while challenges may arise, truth and righteousness will always guide us through the darkest of times."

His confidence and patience did not last.

The coming days would test the mayor's tenuous grip on power as the long-oppressed people of St. Anne revolted against the forces that had poisoned their paradise for far too long.

Paul watched from the shadows, satisfied to see the fire he had lit was now consuming all in its path. Rumors swirled that the mayor was losing what remained of his fragile control. Behind closed doors, his rage and panic knew no bounds. All his years of corruption and misdeeds were now laid bare for the world to see.

Mayor Harris paced his office like a caged animal, lashing out at anyone unlucky enough to cross his path. Only his most ruthless enforcers dared to enter, awaiting orders from their unraveling boss.

"I want whoever is behind this leak found, now!" he spat vehemently. "Turn this whole damn island upside down if you have to. Bring me their heads!"

His men nodded solemnly, very much aware failure was not an option. They had too much of their own blood on their hands to allow any witnesses to exist. As night fell once more, a sinister atmosphere gripped the town. Hit squads took to the streets and jungle trails, stopping at nothing to fulfill their deranged assignment and eliminate all who threatened to topple the crumbling regime.

The mayor's hit squads were like shadows in the night, moving with lethal intent. Their mission was clear: to silence any whispers of dissent and eradicate any trace of opposition to the mayor's reign of corruption. Armed with dark purpose and no regard for life, these ruthless enforcers prowled the streets like predators. They struck swiftly and without mercy, targeting anyone who dared to challenge the mayor's stronghold. Their methods were brutal, leaving fear and bloodshed in their wake.

With cold precision, they hunted down those who dared to speak out, disappearing them into the night with chilling efficiency. Their actions sent a clear message to all who crossed the mayor's path, defy him, and you would pay the price, vanish without a trace, just like the others who dared to stand against him.

It was a harrowing sight to witness; the town gripped by a shadow of terror as the hit squads carried out their grim task. But in the chaos and danger, there were whispers of resistance, of a growing determination to bring the truth to light and put an end to the mayor's tyranny once and for all.

Paul and Mackenzie's lives were now forfeit in the mayor's demented attempt to salvage the tattered threads of power through terror and brutality. The hunt was on for the whistleblowers, and the island's shadows had never seemed more foreboding or dangerous.

Paul peered through the dense foliage, scanning for any signs of movement. With the mayor's squads now combing the island, he and Mackenzie were forced to abandon all their hideouts and vanish off the grid.

"Looks like we've ruffled a few feathers, Mackenzie. The mayor's henchmen are on our trail, and we need to disappear for a while," Paul said, his voice low and serious.

Mackenzie nodded, her eyes reflecting determination and concern. "Agreed, Paul. We can't risk getting caught in the mayor's web. But where do you suggest we lay low?"

He rubbed his chin thoughtfully, weighing their options. "We need a place off the grid, somewhere they won't think to look. How about the old lighthouse on the other side of the island? It's been abandoned for years, but it still offers shelter and a vantage point to keep an eye on our pursuers."

Mackenzie's eyes lit up with a hint of excitement. "That just might work. Plus, it's far enough from the city to give us some breathing room."

And just like that, they set their plan in motion, leaving behind the familiar streets of St. Anne for the solitude and mystery of the abandoned lighthouse, where they would bide their time until the storm passed. In times like these, trust in each other and a quick, decisive plan were their best weapons against the looming threat that shadowed their every move.

Night had fallen once more as they slipped through the wilderness, guided only by the pale moon and their instincts. All traces of their investigation had been erased, with what remained of the documents encrypted and stored online.

The air was heavy with anticipation as Mackenzie and Paul set out on their journey to the abandoned lighthouse. Shadows seemed to stretch out like ghostly fingers along the overgrown path leading to their sanctuary. As they trudged through the wilderness, the rustling of leaves and the distant cry of a lone bird filled the silence between them.

Mackenzie glanced at Paul, a determined glint in her eyes. "Paul, do you think we'll make it to the lighthouse without being followed?"

He adjusted the strap of his bag, his gaze scanning their surroundings. "We'll have to be cautious, Mackenzie. Trust your instincts and keep an eye out for any signs of trouble."

The fading light painted the world in shades of amber and violet, a surreal backdrop to their clandestine journey.

The path ahead grew more rugged, the sound of crashing waves growing louder with each step. Finally, through the thicket of trees, the silhouette of the lighthouse loomed in the distance, a beacon of solitude. As they approached, the towering structure stood like a silent sentinel against the backdrop of the darkening sky. Mackenzie breathed a sigh of relief, her hand reaching out to touch the cold stone.

"We made it, Paul. This will be our refuge for now."

Paul nodded, a sense of grim determination settling over him. "We'll keep watch through the night. The mayor's men won't find us here, not if we're alert." And with that, they settled into their temporary sanctuary, ready to face whatever challenges awaited them in the shadows of the night.

The tension hung heavy in the air like a storm waiting to break. Mackenzie, with her eyes reflecting determination and fear, was a stark reminder of the peril they faced. The soft glow of flashlights illuminated the walls of the lighthouse, casting eerie shadows that matched the uncertainty in their hearts.

As they huddled in that makeshift sanctuary, the silence seemed to amplify the weight of their situation. Mackenzie's voice, usually steady and composed, betrayed a subtle quiver, a raw edge born from the dangers that lurked outside their fragile haven. Her words were measured yet laced with an undercurrent of urgency, a shared understanding of the dire circumstances that bound them together in that dark refuge.

Paul could sense her fear, a primal instinct that whispered of imminent danger. Yet, beneath that fear, there was a flicker of resolve, a silent promise to stand firm in the face of adversity. Paul and Mackenzie's whispered conversation echoed off the damp walls, threading a fragile connection between us, a bond forged in the crucible of danger.

He turned to Mackenzie with calm reassurance, his voice a steady anchor in a storm of uncertainty.

"Mackenzie, fear has a way of clouding our judgment. We must trust in our training, in our instincts, and in each other. We've faced dangers before, and we'll face this one with the same resolve."

Mackenzie, her eyes reflected gratitude and determination, nodded in silent agreement. Her response was a quiet affirmation, a flicker of unwavering trust in their partnership forged through shared dangers.

She spoke softly, her voice carrying a note of newfound courage, "I'm with you, Paul. We'll weather this storm together, no matter what comes our way."

In that brief exchange of words, a bond strengthened by adversity unfurled between them, a bond that transcended the fear that threatened to engulf them. Together, they strengthened their resolve, ready for the challenges that awaited outside the safety of their sanctuary, ready to face whatever dangers the night had in store with a unity born of shared purpose and unshakable resolve.

In those moments of uncertainty and fear, Mackenzie's courage shone through, casting aside the shadows of doubt. Together, they readied for the storm that raged outside, knowing that survival depended not only on skills as investigators but on the unwavering trust they had placed in each other.

As Mackenzie stood guard, Paul booted his laptop, hoping for an Internet connection, and accessed the anonymous Dropbox. Uploads had continued throughout each night, with more incriminating files leaked to keep pressure mounting.

Pictures of illegal weapon stashes. Details of payoffs to judges and officials. Names, dates, and places painted an ever-grimier portrait of corruption on the island. As long as they drew breath, the truth would not stay buried.

Dawn brought no signs they'd been tracked to this remote hideaway.

After a meager meal, they set out once more, knowing their survival depended on staying unseen, for now their fight would continue from the shadows. Justice was still coming, no matter the odds or dangers they faced alone in the oppressive jungle wilds.

The pressure continued mounting on the mayor as more incriminating leaks surfaced each day. Support within city hall was crumbling as his allies scrambled to distance themselves from impending indictments. The mayor's grip on power had never seemed more tenuous. Every move he made was met with protest; every public appearance was jeered by angry crowds demanding resignation. Justice was closing in no matter which way he turned.

In a privately called meeting with his most trusted enforcers, the thin veneer of control finally shattered. "I want those meddling pests erased once and for all," he spat venomously. "Phillips and that female cop are the ones pulling the strings from the shadows. Without them, this whole house of cards will collapse."

Nods and murmurs affirmed around the table. Failure would not be accepted this time. "Take whatever you need. Money, guns, men, it doesn't matter. Just find him and tie up this loose end permanently." With those final instructions, Paul's death warrant was signed. The mayor's order transformed manhunting squads into roaming executioners, leaving a stain of blood on their trail as they scoured the island without mercy or limitations.

Deep in the unforgiving jungle, Paul's and Mackenzie's skills and cunning would be put to the ultimate test while evading those tasked with ending their lives. The hunt had become personal, survival his sole mission against an enemy with nothing left to lose.

As word of the mayor's ruthlessness spread, anger throughout the island swelled into outrage, and citizens who had suffered the corruption's effects for years were spurred to action.

Crowds poured into the streets, brandishing signs decrying the injustices exposed by Paul's leaks. Chants of "Justice for Jane!" and "Harris resign!" echoed off storefronts shuttered in solidarity. Grandmothers shook fists from porches while fishermen abandoned their docks, joining surging protest lines that crippled traffic. Students marched with teachers as mutual distrust in authorities united generations.

Attempts to contain demonstrations only galvanized further participation. Police in riot gear found themselves facing off against everyday people, neighbors, and even families. Loyalties are fractured under moral pressure. By nightfall, a general strike had brought the island's economy to a standstill. Buildings were plastered with flyers naming co-conspirators in acts that shocked the conscious. No one in power seemed safe from rising public ire.

Only truth and nonviolence could see residents through the darkness, but momentum was theirs to shape the destiny waiting at the revolution's precipice. The people had found their voice at last.

Mayor Harris paced his office like a caged animal, the walls closing in around his crumbling regime. Outside, protests showed no signs of abating as demands for justice reached fever pitch. When the phone buzzed, he snatched it up eagerly, hoping for news the meddlesome Phillips and Mackenzie had been dealt with. Instead, his lieutenant's grave tone confirmed the opposite; manhunts had turned up nothing in the dense jungle's vastness.

Swearing violently, Harris punched the desk, oblivious to the splintering pain in his bloodied knuckles. Ruin was coming down around him, and former partners in crime were the first rats to flee the sinking ship. Word had come that thugs like Cole and Delgado were purging incriminating evidence, distancing themselves from the tangled web of corruption the mayor could no longer protect.

Without leverage over the law, his authority meant nothing to hardened criminals.

Even bribery could no longer sway those pledged to take him down. Kim Wong's story had been picked up internationally, lighting a fuse to scandals the mayor couldn't hope to contain. Global scrutiny was turning St. Anne into a dictator state. Jane read every word from Sanctuary on Guadalupe with glee. For the first time in a very long time, a smile was showing on her face.

Resignation crept into Harris' unhinged ranting. Paul's maddening victory was now complete, he had toppled a tyrant's reign through nonviolence and truth alone. All that remained was to watch the ruins crumble into the ashes of his legacy.

Deep in the forbidding jungle night, Paul and Mackenzie took stock of their dire situation. Their campaign had succeeded beyond any expectation, yet bringing down a regime meant exposure in its death throes. Gathered close by flickering candlelight, they watched graphic videos uploaded covertly; protestors bloodied, homes ransacked in violence sanctioned by a regime with nothing left to lose.

The mayor's henchmen were feral beasts, unchained at last. "We started a revolution, but it will die if things escalate much further," Paul murmured grimly. Mackenzie nodded, exhausted yet resolved. "The people need proof the conspiracy goes right to the top before true change can begin."

A plan took shape: infiltrate the heart of the beast one final time to obtain the smoking gun crucial to ushering in peace and democracy. "It will be the most dangerous move we've made so far," Paul acknowledged softly.

Mackenzie met his steady gaze, unafraid. "We do this together, or not at all. Our destiny remains the same: to lift this shadow and let the light in, whatever it costs."

Around them, the jungle stirred ominously, yet in each other, they found courage for whatever lay ahead.

Dawn would bring the culmination of their joint campaign.

Fates hung in precarious balance along with the future of the island they had come to love so well despite its darkness. For justice and St. Anne, there could be no other choice but to face the enemy one last time.

Paul and Mackenzie settled into an uneasy sleep, knowing morning could bring their final battle. As the last embers of fire faded, their fates drifted in and out of fitful dreams. Mackenzie tossed uneasily, reliving proud moments that brought them to this pass, Jane's light nearly snuffed out, ordinary souls robbed of hope under corruption's boot. Paul dreamed of jungle shadows closing in, hunters with death in their smiles emerging from the mist.

A mournful howl in the distance pulled them from haunted visions. Dark circles ringed steely eyes as they chewed a somber dawn meal, knowing this day would destroy or fulfill their mission's vow.

Dawn had arrived.

Without words, they checked equipment one final time, files, devices, and crude weapons to even slim odds against foes with nothing left but bloodlust. Rising as the first rays filtered through the canopy, they prepared to face what fate decreed.

Paul advised Mackenzie to tread carefully but stay resolute in seeking the truth. He emphasized the importance of staying one step ahead of their enemies and using their overconfidence against them. Mackenzie's response was concern for the risks involved but also a newfound determination to see this through to the end. Paul feels she is starting to understand the depth of corruption they're up against and the sacrifices they must make to bring justice to light. It will be a tough road ahead, but he had faith in her growing resolve.

Paul leaned in and spoke in hushed tones, outlining the dangers that lay ahead.

"Shadows lurk in every corner of our investigation, waiting to strike at any moment." Paul could see the flicker of uncertainty in her eyes, but beneath that uncertainty, there was a glimmer of steel determination. "The only way to combat this evil is with unwavering courage, that our pursuit of truth must be stronger than the deepest secrets we are going to uncover."

Mackenzie listened intently, her expression shifting from doubt to a silent acceptance of the risks that came with this treacherous game we were playing.

At that moment, Paul knew she was beginning to grasp the gravity of the mission, the gravity of standing against those who sought to bury the truth. And as she nodded, a silent agreement passed between them, a pact to face whatever challenges came their way, united in the pursuit of justice.

Shouldering their packs, Paul and Mackenzie looked to the veil of trees cloaking their fateful destination where enemies and destinies would collide. With steady hands and thunderous hearts, they strode into the yawning green not as a hunter and hunted but as two united against injustice wherever it hid its hideous face.

This, the conclusion they had been marching toward since taking their united stand. In the jungle's shrouded depths, light and shadows would wrestle for St. Anne's soul, and their own, in the climactic battle to come.

CHAPTER ELEVEN

Confronting the Beast

WITH DETERMINATION IN HIS EYES, PAUL EXAMINED THE collection of evidence spread out before him one final time. Every incriminating document, photograph, and recording reinforced his resolution. It was time for the mayor and his corrupt regime to be unmasked for the entire island to see.

When evening fell and the nighttime skies became dark, Paul crept towards the grand manor that had come to symbolize the oppression gripping St. Anne. His breath slowed as he expertly bypassed the security patrols. He knew that every half-hour, the security guards would do their rounds, and that was his window of opportunity.

Paul peered into the mayor's rich office through an open window.

Mahogany desks adorned with gilded frames and shelves lined with leather-bound books masking darker agendas dominated the room. The air was heavy with the scent of privilege and deceit, where every polished surface gleamed with false authority. It's a facade of wealth built upon the crumbling foundation of corruption. The very walls seem to echo whispers of hidden deals and broken promises.

There, the man sat, still confident in the shadowy protection of his ill-gotten power. As if summoned, two well-dressed men entered to confer privately with the mayor. Paul activated the recording device in his pocket and listened intently.

"The dissidents are growing bolder. They must be silenced before the whole system comes crashing down," one advisor remarked. At this confirmation of criminality, Paul felt his evidence was secure. He emerged from the shadows.

Gaining entry into the mayor's house was a delicate operation. After overhearing the conversation through the window, Paul had to act swiftly but cautiously. With his background in investigations, picking a lock or two wasn't much trouble. Once inside, it was all about presenting the evidence calmly yet assertively. There's a certain satisfaction in seeing the truth laid bare in front of those who thought they could hide behind their lies. Justice may be blind, but it sure has a way of finding its target.

Moving from the back door to the mayor's office undetected was like navigating a labyrinth of shadows and secrets. The night was draped in an inky silence, broken only by the occasional rustle of leaves in the cool breeze. Paul moved with the precision of a ghost, his steps light and purposeful. Lights from nearby rooms cast a dim glow, guiding him through the maze of hallways and corridors.

The office loomed ahead like a fortress. As he approached, the adrenaline coursing through his veins heightened his senses, sharpening his focus. Every creak of the floorboards, every whisper of the curtains seemed amplified in the stillness of the night. He felt like a lone wolf stalking its prey, determined and unyielding.

With each step closer to the office, the weight of anticipation hung heavy in the air. The moment of truth awaited beyond those closed doors, where secrets would be laid bare and lies exposed. It was a dance of shadows and light, stealth, and revelation, culminating in a confrontation that would shape the course of justice itself. And as Paul stood outside that office, ready to confront the mayor with his evidence, he knew that the truth, like a beacon in the night, would prevail.

"The system has already fallen," Paul declared, bursting through the mayor's office door, brandishing the damning files. Shock and rage swept over the mayor's face in turn. "You're finished," Paul said steadily. "Call off your goons and turn yourself into the authorities, or this evidence goes public."

A tense standoff ensued, the fate of St. Anne hanging in the balance.

The mayor scrambled for some remnant of power but found himself cornered at last in his web of deceit. As Paul confronted corruption within the manor, deadly threats closed in from without.

While Paul was entering the mayor's office, Mackenzie was keeping watch from a vantage point just outside the window. Perched like a silent sentinel, she scanned the surroundings with an eagle eye, ensuring that no unexpected visitors or unwanted interruptions would disrupt our quest for justice. With her keen instincts and unwavering loyalty, Mackenzie was the perfect ally in our pursuit of the truth.

Together, they formed a formidable team, each playing their part in unraveling the mysteries that lay before them. Her presence was not just reassuring; it was essential in their mission to uncover the secrets that the mayor sought to keep hidden.

She was vigilantly tracking any signs of the mayor's enforcers stirring in the night. Her senses prickled as a crack of twigs snapped behind her position. Spinning swiftly, she saw only darkness. Still, an ominous instinct warned of lurking eyes.

She quickened her pace towards the rear door of the mayor's house and Paul. As she neared the door, a looming figure appeared from seemingly from nowhere.

"The mayor sends his regards," a gruff voice growled.

Mackenzie drew her weapon, but it was knocked aside as two more assailants emerged. She struggled against their brutal grips as a blade flashed under the moonlight. Not here, not like this, she thought desperately. A shot rang out, and her attackers froze, then collapsed dead with perfect shots to the head.

Mackenzie turned to see a hooded stranger lowering a smoking rifle.

"Paul needs backup. The mayor has lost all restraint," the figure said, voice muffled. Nodding thanks, Mackenzie ran towards the confrontation, alive but more resolved than ever to see justice done.

Mackenzie recognized the stranger who intervened. He was a local fisherman named Jacques. A brave soul, she thought, willing to risk his safety to help me in my time of need. Quite the unexpected ally,

The corrupt regime's days were numbered.

Paul sensed the danger before he heard the shots ring out. Gripping his pistol and the evidence, he ran down the hallway and slipped out of the rear exit just as a vehicle roared into the driveway. Four large men emerged purposefully, weapons drawn.

"Find them," the mayor growled into the darkness.

Mackenzie and Paul made a hasty escape from the mayor's house. As they dashed away into the cool night air, adrenaline still coursing through their veins, a sense of triumph and satisfaction washed over them.

Mackenzie kept pace beside Paul, her presence a steady reassurance in the chaos of our flight. The night sky was a tapestry of stars, watching over us like silent guardians as we made our escape.

As they were running through the dense jungle, Paul was aware they were being followed. They stopped at a large, very old oak tree to catch their breath. Just then, they heard the mayor's men coming after them. They were only 20 yards away and closing!

Leaping from cover, Paul struck the first man hard across the face as he approached the tree, grabbing his fallen weapon in one fluid motion. Shouts rose as the others spotted him, uncapping the triggers on their automatic weapons.

Darting between the dense trees, Paul and Mackenzie returned suppressive fire while maintaining stealthful evasion. A staccato of shots chipped bark all around, yet none found their marks. Enraged, two pursuers closed in from either side, hoping to pin them down. Paul doubled back and emerged behind his stalkers through the camouflage.

As they spun in panic too slowly, two precise shots felled each man where they stood. Only the leader remained, wide eyes glistening beneath his balaclava in the moonlight. With the tables now turned, Paul emerged from the brush, gun leveled.

"Call off your friends or join them," he said calmly but firmly.

The stage was set for the final showdown. Justice will be delivered tonight. Paul took quick stock of their surroundings as Mackenzie emerged from behind the oak tree. Three more assailants had arrived from the mayor's house, encircling Paul and Mackenzie to cut off any escape route through the dense jungle growth. They were outnumbered but not yet beaten.

Paul listened carefully to the footfalls closing in, counting the steps to gauge their positions. When the time was right, he signaled to Mackenzie to strike. Launching from the shadows, Paul dropped the nearest enemy with a downward elbow strike to the spine. He seized the man's weapon before the others could retaliate while Mackenzie fired with precision, unleashing a spray of covering fire into the bushes.

Bullets ripped through the foliage as they rolled to another hiding spot. They listened again as the hitmen regrouped, narrowing in on their position.

"Let them come to us," he whispered to Mackenzie, readying an ambush.

The first moved in too hastily and met a knife hand to the throat. As the man gagged, Paul grabbed his body as a shield, exchanging fire with the final assailant at close range.

When the weapon clicked empty, Paul hurled his improvised guard and leaped. A brutal brawl ensued under the pale moon.

Through tactical use of terrain and experience, Paul methodically wore down his larger opponent. In the end, the man collapsed, finally outmatched. The jungle fell silent once more.

Paul took a moment to catch his breath. Their enemies were defeated, but the war remained yet to be won. Wiping the sweat from his brow, they pushed on into the night. Paul surveyed the fallen bodies, ensuring none would rise again.

As they turned to depart, a twig snapped behind them. They spun just in time to see a masked assailant emerge from the shadows. Paul fired, but his weapon clicked empty. With a growled curse, the man was on him. They crashed to the earth, exchanging brutal blows.

Paul felt ribs crack but fought on, hand scrabbling for a weapon. His fingers found purchase on a fallen knife. He struck, feeling flesh part beneath the blade. Yet his opponent seized Paul's wrist and twisted, eliciting a scream of agony. The knife fell as his arm went numb. A meaty crunch echoed as the man headbutted Paul, bursting his nose.

As stars exploded across Paul's vision as he was rolled onto his back, he heard the shot from Mackenzie's gun. Paul's assailant dropped, never to see another day.

With that, Paul collapsed, consciousness fading. Their work was not yet done, but his body had nothing left to give. As darkness closed in, his last thoughts were of the battle still to come and ensuring justice for St. Anne. With his last ounce of will, Paul fought against the creeping darkness. Mackenzie dragged Paul as he tried to walk himself across damp soil, leaving a snail's trail of blood behind him. His shattered body demanded rest, but his spirit would not surrender while justice remained undone.

Chest heaving, he collapsed back into the waiting embrace of jungle humus. His task was complete, though his own life now hung by a thread. Satisfied, he was about to surrender to darkness. His war was won.

Several minutes later, with his enemies defeated, Paul forced himself to rise on unsteady legs as Mackenzie placed her arm around Paul's waist. Each ragged breath was a battle against the growing crimson inside. But he would not rest while St. Anne remained at risk.

Leaning heavily upon Mackenzie for support, Paul began a limping march towards the manor, leaving a small trail of blood behind him. His movements were slow and unsteady yet driven by fierce determination.

As the manor came into view through the thinning trees, Mackenzie told Paul to wait while she went ahead to assess the situation at the mayor's house.

A few minutes after she left, gunshots rang out. His adrenaline surged, momentarily dulling Paul's agony as he lurched towards the shots during a painful run. Breaking into a small clearing, Paul spotted two large men converging on Mackenzie's small form in the darkness.

She battled fiercely but was clearly overwhelmed. With a primal roar of rage, Paul drew the attention of the nearer attacker. His fists met flesh with punishing force, driving the man back. Mackenzie turned the moment to her advantage, disarming her own opponent in confusion. Together, they made short work of the remaining threats.

"We have to move, now!" Paul rasped urgently through clenched teeth. Mackenzie's eyes widened at his condition, but she did not hesitate. Together they fled into the jungle toward allies who could tend their wounds, putting distance between themselves and the crimes of the mayor at last.

With pursuers closing in, Paul pulled Mackenzie deeper into the dense jungle cover. Their flight was hampered by his many wounds, yet adrenaline surged them onwards despite the agony. Behind them crashed the stomping boots of hired guns, merciless in their hunt. Paul knew one glancing shot would spell their ends, but pushing

Mackenzie ahead, he laid down suppressing fire to shield their escape.

The tropical terrain battered their weary frames. Thorns scored flesh as they plunged through the clingy brush. Paul's vision swam, yet he dared not to slow, dragging himself on through sheer force of will. At last, their haven appeared ahead, but so did a looming silhouette blocking their path.

Paul cried a warning as Mackenzie skidded to a halt, backtracking hurriedly from the raised weapon. With a wordless snarl, Paul launched himself, meeting death in a grappling tumble amid the tangled flora. Mackenzie pounced to aid Paul in the fray, wresting the gun aside to aim into shadowed faces pursuing.

Shots echoed as Paul subdued their final obstacle. Together, they then fled anew into sheltering trees, their pursuers falling back. At last, the jungle muffled all signs of pursuit, and they collapsed in shared relief and anguish.

The battle was over, but the war remained to be seen through to its conclusion. Paul slumped against a gnarled trunk, every ragged breath an agony. Darkness clawed at his vision once more as warm blood seeped the earth.

"Stay with me!" Mackenzie's anguished voice echoed from far away. Her hands pressed futile dressings to his pulpy flesh, slowing the blood loss as best she could. Through the haze, Paul heard an ominous sound carried on the breeze, engines revving, and dogs baying as the hunt redoubled its efforts. Their pursuers had tracked them even to this hidden glade. There would be no escape.

Summoning his last shreds of strength, Paul gripped Mackenzie's arm urgently. "Go...warn others. Can't...let them die in vain." But she would not be moved, clinging tighter still as fresh tears fell upon his ashen face.

"Please...you can't leave me too." Her broken plea pierced the fog more sharply than any blade. Paul coughed weakly in reply, fingers clasping hers with a reassurance he did not feel. Darkness swirled, gluttonous to claim its prize.

As the encroaching sounds of doom neared, Paul's eyes fluttered shut once more. Whether it was the final slumber or a chance to rise again, fate would decide beyond the veil drawing closed...

Paul and Mackenzie's fates hung in the balance as enemies closed their noose once more in the gathering gloom. Victory or ruin now seemed turned upon a knife edge for St. Anne's souls still fighting in the shadows, leaving Paul's fate uncertain as enemies close in once more.

CHAPTER TWELVE

Edge of the Abyss

BATTERED AND BLOODIED, PAUL SAT AGAINST A TREE, STILL TRYING TO catch his breath. His shoulder ached where the bullet had grazed him. He had lost Mackenzie as they split up on their flight through the jungle and could only hope she had managed to escape to retrieve back. Gritting his teeth, he pushed off the tree and continued stumbling through the dense foliage.

The darkness of night made it even harder to see. But he knew these woods like the back of his hand and used that knowledge now to stay one step ahead of his pursuers. Their shouts and flashlight beams hinted that the mayor's men were growing closer. Paul had to finish this and finish it now before they overtook him. He changed course, circling back toward the last place he had heard their voices.

As he neared the edge of the trees, two dark figures emerged in the distance. Paul watched them for a moment, recognizing the heavyset silhouettes of the mayor and one of his lackeys.

Drawing the gun Mackenzie had left with him, with a shaking hand, Paul staggered out of the foliage. "Mayor Harris!" he yelled hoarsely. The two men whirled with a start. Before they could react, Paul aimed his gun at the mayor's head.

"Call off your dogs," he growled, "or I'll end you right here." Fear flickered in the mayor's eyes as he raised his hands. He nodded to his companion, who withdrew a radio.

"Stand down," the mayor muttered between clenched teeth. "We've got what we came for."

Paul grabbed the mayor by the collar, pressing the gun harder against his temple. At last, he had the man who had ruined so many lives at his mercy. And he was finally going to get some answers. Paul forced the mayor toward the edge of the clearing, keeping the gun trained on him.

"Tell me why you tried to kill Jane," he growled.

The mayor sneered. "That meddlesome bank manager? She got what was coming to her."

Rage boiled in Paul's veins. "Who hurt her?"

"Ask Cole," the mayor spat. "He took care of the problem."

The mayor truly thought Jane was dead, not knowing she survived, and was now hiding safely on another island, ready to testify against him. But Paul would still make these men pay.

"You're finished here," he said. "I have enough evidence now to bury you." A sinister smile curled the mayor's lips.

"Do you really think it's that simple? I'm just a small piece in something much larger."

Paul pressed the gun harder against the mayor's temple. "Explain. Now."

The mayor chuckled. "There are forces at play you can't understand. This island is just a waystation, a hub for our operations throughout the Caribbean. You could tear me down, but another would simply take my place. The machine will keep turning with or without me."

It was worse than Paul imagined. Corruption flowed through the entire Caribbean like rot. But he had to try. "Spare me your rationalizations. I want names, dates, and full details of every crime. You're going to bring this whole rotten structure down from the inside." Fear entered the mayor's eyes again. For the first time, Paul saw a glimmer of hope. He had leverage at last.

Paul's grip on the gun tightened as the mayor began to speak. "Jane put up a fight," he said darkly. "But Cole wanted to send a message, so he made it slow."

Bile rose in Paul's throat at the cruel delight in the mayor's voice. "Tell me everything, he growled through clenched teeth."

The mayor looked past Paul into the jungle as if remembering. "Cole's boys grabbed her as she left the bank one night. Took her to the old quarry. By the time Cole was done with her, she could hardly beg for death." Paul saw Jane's torment play out in his mind, the terror and agony she must have endured. His finger tensed on the trigger.

As if sensing Paul's rage, the mayor hastily added, "That's just business. Nothing personal, you understand. This island runs how I say. Anyone who steps out of line gets the same as Jane."

Rage and grief battled within Paul. He longed to pull the trigger and end this vile man. But justice had to be served properly. He could not wait until Jane walked into the courtroom to testify against the mayor. Paul could only imagine the look on the mayor's face.

With a trembling hand, he grabbed the mayor's radio. "To all units," he said coldly. "Stand down. Return to base immediately. Your mayor and I have unfinished matters to discuss."

As footsteps retreated in the woods, Paul stared death at the mayor. "Now it's your turn," he said quietly. "I want the whole truth, and then you'll face justice for your crimes." Paul listened as the mayor spilled every gruesome detail of corruption on the island. Names. Dates. Crimes. It was enough to put away every criminal in the network.

Exhausted, Paul lowered the gun. "Your fate is sealed," he told Harris. "Justice will be served."

A deranged grin spread on the mayor's face. "You think it will be that easy? My friends won't let me face the chair alone." As if on cue, an engine roared in the darkness. Headlights burst through the trees as an armored vehicle barreled toward them.

Paul shoved the mayor aside and lifted his gun, but it was no use. He was out outmatched. The vehicle skidded to a stop, and armed men poured out. "Easy boys," the mayor laughed. "Our friend and I were just having a chat." Paul backed toward the trees, frantically searching for an escape. But the jungle was alien in the dark, and the men closed in with eager bloodlust.

He had to make a run for it. With an agonized groan, Paul turned and bolted into the gloom. Gunfire and shouts erupted behind him as the pursuit began. He had the truth, but surviving would take every ounce of strength and cunning he had left. Paul crashed through the undergrowth, ignoring the knives of pain stabbing through his injured body. He had to escape and hope Mackenzie was bringing help.

Slowing to a walk, he pulled out his knife and began spreading false trails. He doubled back and circled, creating false tracks to confuse his pursuers. Years of hunting in woods like these served him well now. As dawn lit the sky, Paul paused to catch his breath. He wiped the blade clean and continued following a creek upstream.

Soon, he came upon the pitiful shelter they had built empty.

Panic rose in his chest until he spotted fresh signs. Mackenzie had passed this way just hours ago, heading north toward their rendezvous point. Paul renewed his pace. At midday, he crested a ridge and saw a familiar stand of mangroves in the distance. As he approached, a figure rose from the shadows, rifle raised.

"Mackenzie," he rasped. She lowered the rifle and rushed to his side, arm beneath his shoulders. She looked at Paul with a steadfast gaze and said, "I'm glad you're safe, Paul. We've come too far to let them win now. We'll see this through, no matter what it takes."

"I couldn't leave you Paul. I knew you would make it here, so I waited. The jungle is full of the mayor's men", she said with tears forming.

Her voice held a firm resolve, a commitment to the cause they both believed in. It was a silent vow between them, an unspoken agreement to stand together against the forces of corruption that sought to destroy everything held dear. In that moment, her words echoed with a sense of unity and purpose, propelling them forward into the heart of darkness with unwavering courage and conviction.

Mackenzie's eyes revealed relief at seeing Paul alive, worry for what was to come, and a steely resolve that mirrored Paul's.

Their conversation was brief but intense. They exchanged a silent nod, a mutual acknowledgment of the risks that they had faced and the challenges that lay ahead. Mackenzie shared how she managed to slip away from her captors, using her quick thinking and resourcefulness to evade them.

"Where have you been hiding?" Paul asked.

"In an abandoned fishing shack by the cliffs, waiting for the perfect moment to break free and come back to find you."

Despite the dangers that loomed, there was a sense of camaraderie at that moment, a shared understanding of the perilous path they had chosen to walk together.

As Paul gazed out at the darkening horizon, the weight of the mission pressed upon them, pushing them forward with a renewed determination to see justice served, no matter the cost. And in that fleeting moment of respite, Paul knew that Mackenzie had proven herself a steadfast ally, ready to face whatever challenges awaited us in the final act of our battle against corruption.

As they rested, they made final preparations. Using Paul's local knowledge, they gathered supplies and booby-trapped false trails to deter pursuit. Soon, they would vanish into the jungle once more and move on to the next stage of survival. Justice was still out of reach, but their lives remained. For now, that would have to be enough.

Together, they pushed through the dense jungle, navigating by the dying light of the sunset. Their injuries slowed them, but they knew resting would mean death.

They began setting more traps around their camp. But unease gnawed at Paul. The hunters were too close, closing off potential escape routes. His fears were confirmed just before dawn. Distant explosions rumbled through the trees, followed by the crackle of flames.

Looking back, they saw a burning glow on the horizon. "They're burning the jungle," Mackenzie gasped.

Terror gripped Paul's heart as he realized their trap was now complete. Fire would force them into the open, where bullets awaited. As smoke billowed their way, Paul racked his brain for an exit. The shore was miles away, and every path was blocked. They were cornered rats with no way out.

A grim idea took form. "We'll have to fight our way through. Lay down what traps remain, and let's pray it gives us an edge." Mackenzie's weary eyes hardened.

They readied themselves for what they thought would be the final confrontation, knowing this may be the end of the line. Death or justice, there was no turning back now.

The hunters closed in, and all Paul and Mackenzie could do was stand their ground. With flames crackling behind them, Paul strained his mind for any scrap of an idea. They huddled in the meager shelter, listening to the hunters draw nearer through the dense smoke.

As the flames from the spreading fire crept closer to their hiding spot, the air grew thick with acrid smoke, and the crackling of burning wood filled the night. The glow of the fire cast eerie shadows around Paul and Mackenzie, painting the landscape in a surreal light that danced with the flickering flames.

The heat became oppressive, searing against their skin and sending waves of discomfort through their tired bodies. Embers whirled in the air like fiery spirits, carried by the heated drafts that spiraled around. The roar of the inferno grew louder, a menacing symphony of destruction that seemed to swallow all other sounds.

Mackenzie and Paul exchanged a glance, eyes reflecting fear and determination as they braced for what was to come. The encroaching fire painted a picture of imminent danger, a relentless force of nature that cared not for their struggles or mission. In that moment of impending chaos, they strengthened themselves against the surge of flames, ready to confront whatever challenges the fiery onslaught brought our way.

"We need a diversion," Paul muttered. His eyes fell on an old hunting trap, long discarded in the ruins of the shelter. An idea took shape. "Give me a hand with this." Quickly, they constructed a crude incendiary device from explosives pried from other traps that they had laid.

Paul handed Mackenzie a pistol. "When it blows, run in the other direction. I'll draw them off."

Mackenzie shook her head fiercely. "No, it's too dangerous. We go together or not at all."

Coughing from the smoke, Paul grasped her shoulders. "Have faith in me. I need to buy us time to escape. Now go, and don't look back."

Reluctantly, she melted into the smoky jungle as Paul activated the trap. A thunderous blast shook the trees, followed by shouting men. Paul bolted in the opposite direction, firing into the smoke.

Behind him, boots pounded in pursuit. But had Mackenzie managed to slip away? Paul prayed she had reached safety as bullets whizzed past. He was the bait, and the hunters were taking it, buying Mackenzie the time she needed to disappear into the shadows of the burning forest. Now, he just had to survive long enough for his strategy to work.

Paul crashed through the burning undergrowth as bullets whipped past. The smoke choked him and seared his lungs. He had to lead his pursuers farther away to give Mackenzie a chance at escape.

Spotting a clearing up ahead, Paul darted sideways into thicker foliage. He doubled back silently and circled, watching from the tree line as armed men charged past his former position, oblivious to his trick. He took a moment to regain his breath.

The crackle of flames drew nearer; time was running out. He set off on a painful jog parallel to the clearing, knowing any trail could yield pursuers. Suddenly, a trap snapped ahead. Paul dove aside as a figure tumbled out with a cry, clothes aflame. In moments, the man was engulfed, screaming horribly until death silenced him.

With his heart pounding, Paul crept on. Deeper in the burning forest, Mackenzie paused amid the ruins of a shelter, hoping for a sign of Paul's survival. A faint cry carried on the smoke, spurring her back into flight.

Dusk had fallen as Paul burst onto an eroding beach. Waves lapped the dark sands as flames consumed the jungle behind them. Mackenzie emerged from the tree line and collapsed into his arms. Their pursuers were lost in the smoke and fire, the inferno hiding their escape at last.

Justice remained out of reach, but for now, survival would have to be enough. Exhausted but determined, Paul and Mackenzie reunited and retreated into the jungle. They knew the mayor's men would be relentlessly combing the coast and paths to the north. Their only chance was to reach the derelict southern docks, avoiding the jungle flames under cover of darkness.

As they crept through the dense brush, Paul saw Mackenzie struggling to suppress her labored breathing. Her injuries were taking their toll. He slung her arm over his shoulders and steadied her steps, forcing himself to ignore his own pain. Justice meant nothing if they didn't survive.

The long hours of night slipped by as they threaded their way along game trails. Just before dawn, they glimpsed lights shimmering through the trees, their target in sight. But as they surveyed the dock from the tree line, Paul's heart sank. Armed figures patrolled the decrepit wharf where their only boat waited.

They were too late. Their escape was blocked once more. Paul searched for alternative routes as Mackenzie rested, her life fading. Their mission had pushed them to the brink. Had it all been for naught?

Paul noticed a gleam of hope, an untended skiff drifting alone in the water. Their fate would be decided here. Either freedom or death awaited in the rolling waters stretching endlessly beyond the breakers' roar. One final stand could secure their escape from this place of oppression and sorrow.

Paul roused Mackenzie, and together, they began their final push through the gauntlet to salvation or the depths. With the last of their strength, Paul and Mackenzie hauled their battered bodies through the clinging mud of the marshy shoreline under dawn's pale light. The skiff rocked in the swells just ahead.

A shout sounded from the docks; they'd been spotted. Paul redoubled his efforts, ignoring the agony coursing through his frame. As boots pounded the wharf, he tumbled with Mackenzie into the skiff and unmoored with shaking hands.

Gunfire cracked across the water as the small boat drifted free. Paul labored with the heavy oars, urging them offshore despite his failing strength. Behind, armed men lined the crumbling docks and swarmed into motorboats, hungry for the kill.

As the pursuers closed in, a hope arose on the horizon ahead. A battered trawler puttered toward the skiff, waving them aboard with calls of aid. Paul collapsed in gratitude as rough hands hauled them over the rail.

At the helm stood a grizzled fisherman, eyes burning with indignation. "The mayor harmed too many good folks," he growled. "Thought ye could use a pickup." Mackenzie recognized the fisherman as Jacques, the same man who saved her near the mayor's house. A man of few words but great courage. His timely intervention turned the tide in Paul's and Mackenzie's favor that day.

Paul clasped the man's arm in thanks as shouted curses arose behind. The last boats were giving chase, guns blazing. But the trawler kicked into gear, plowing a course through the breakers as Paul and Mackenzie clung to life and the justice yet to come.

At long last, escape was theirs. St. Anne and its evil receded into the past, replaced by open waters full of possibility and redemption. Their mission would be fulfilled at last.

CHAPTER THIRTEEN

Fugitives on the Run

THE GENTLE LAPPING OF THE WAVES AGAINST THE SIDE OF THE BOAT was a soothing melody after the cacophony of danger and destruction. The fisherman, a weathered old soul with a kind face, extended a hand to Paul and Mackenzie, offering safety amid the turmoil.

As they boarded the boat, Mackenzie and Paul exchanged words of gratitude and relief with the fisherman. "Our heartfelt thanks for your timely intervention," Paul said to Jaques, acknowledging that his act of kindness had likely saved their lives.

Mackenzie's eyes held a glimmer of exhaustion mixed with gratitude, her shoulders relaxing with the weight lifted off them, if only for a moment.

The saving boat was a medium-sized fishing boat, its paint slightly weathered from battling the elements. The sound of the motor echoed across the water, a comforting roar in the silence of the open sea. The boat's appearance conveyed a sense of reliability, with fishing nets neatly stacked and a seasoned captain at the helm. It was a sight for sore eyes after the ordeal Mackenzie and Paul had endured.

Jaques, with a gruff yet warm smile, nodded in understanding, steering the boat away from the burning shoreline as they sailed toward safety. The cool sea breeze brushed against their faces, carrying with it a sense of freedom and respite from the harrowing ordeal they had just faced.

Mackenzie and Paul shared a silent glance that spoke volumes, a mix of relief, disbelief, and a newfound sense of camaraderie born from surviving the crucible of danger together.

As the boat cut through the tranquil waters, leaving the chaos of the night behind, a wave of emotions washed over both, a blend of exhaustion, gratitude, and a glimmer of hope that whispered of better days to come. In that fleeting moment of respite, they found comfort in each other's presence, united by a shared bond forged in the crucible of adversity.

After the intense escape from the mayor and his henchman, Mackenzie, and Paul decided it was time to retreat and regroup.

Paul turned to the captain with a steady gaze, "Take us to the southern cove, Captain. We need a place that is more secluded than where we have been hiding. That's where we'll find the peace to regroup and replan." The captain nodded, understanding the gravity of their mission, and steered the boat towards the destined haven.

The captain took Paul and Mackenzie to the southern tip of the island, a secluded cove hidden away from prying eyes and turbulent waters. The jungle here was a dense thicket near the base of the island's tallest peak, where the foliage was so thick that sunlight could barely penetrate the canopy.

After being brought to safety by Jacques and his boat and saying their goodbyes, they made their way through the dense jungle once again, evading any prying eyes on shore, seeking safety in the unforgiving yet protective embrace of nature. The jungle has now become their sanctuary as they plan their next move against the corruption that threatened to engulf them.

The jungle foliage provided little shelter from the punishing sun and heat as Paul and Mackenzie pushed further into the wilderness, knowing their pursuers were relentless.

They just didn't know how relentless.

A hail of gunfire shredded leaves mere feet from their position.

As the mayor's men closed in on their concealed sanctuary in the jungle, a sense of surprise mingled with the thrill of the unexpected. Paul and Mackenzie shared a knowing glance, silently acknowledging the inevitable confrontation that lay ahead.

The mayor's henchmen, a shadowy presence looming over the island, have eyes and ears in every corner. They navigate the terrain with a familiarity that hints at a deeper connection to the island's secrets. It wasn't just luck that led them to Paul and Mackenzie in the jungle; it was their pervasive reach and unwavering determination that led them right to their doorstep.

The mayor's influence casts a long shadow indeed.

"Mackenzie, it seems our unwelcome guests have found us," Paul remarked, his tone laced with a hint of resignation.

Mackenzie, ever resilient, replied with determination and defiance, "We knew this day would come, Paul. Let's face them head-on and uncover the truth they're so desperate to hide."

With that unspoken agreement, they braced themselves for the imminent clash with the mayor's men, ready to confront the forces that sought to obscure the truth they were so intent on uncovering.

Mackenzie expressed concern, "How long can we keep up the grueling pace?" Though exhausted, Paul resolved to put distance between themselves and those hunting them.

Staying low and blending with the natural camouflage of their surroundings, they skirted around a hill and came across a narrow stream. Seeing an opportunity, Paul and Mackenzie waded into the cool waters. The current swept them along for several miles as they choked back gasps and focused on controlling their breathing.

Facing danger head-on is part and parcel of seeking justice in a corrupt world. The adrenaline, the urgency, the primal instinct to survive, it's all a part of the game. Giving up had never entered their minds. The pursuit of truth and justice fueled their determination, even amidst the chaos and danger.

Mackenzie and Paul knew they had to keep pressing forward, no matter the cost.

Emerging downstream, they took stock under cover of dense ferns. Multiple sets of bootprints overlapped where their enemies had swept through. Paul and Mackenzie shared a tense look, silently agreeing to press on while they still retained this small advantage.

The pursuit continued, with their very survival hanging by the slimmest of threads. Paul checked the bandage wrapped around Mackenzie's calf. Though he'd done his best to clean and bind the wound, infection was setting in. Their small collection of medical supplies had long since been depleted.

Mackenzie managed a wan smile. "How does the patient fare, doctor?"

"You'll live if that leg holds together." Paul kept his voice light through worry gnawed at him.

She was in no condition for a forced march. Neither was he, for that matter, with his various cuts, burns and bruises. They'd evaded their pursuers this long through grit, guile, and good fortune. But the toll of constant flight was taking its due.

As night fell, Paul and Mackenzie took refuge beneath an immense banyan's shaggy branches. Too exposed to risk having a campfire, they dined on wild figs, a few items from the boat, and what remained in their canteens.

After setting up what few defenses they could muster, Paul tried to rest. But enemy encampments could be heard in the distance, the sounds of many men coordinating a hunt. Sleep would not come easily, with their foes so close.

Dawn would bring further hardship and choices that could seal their fates once and for all. With the moon pale overhead, Paul and Mackenzie staggered through the thick jungle. Mackenzie leaned heavily on Paul, her breath coming in ragged gasps. Ahead, the glow of flashlights preceded drunken shouts and laughter. A patrol of the mayor's men approached with weapons slack in their grip. Drunk on their supposed easy victory, they'd let their guard down.

Laying Mackenzie down as gently as he could, Paul drew his knife and circled soundlessly through the dense growth. Emerging behind the rearmost man, his blade found its home between his shoulder blades.

Chaos erupted as rifles came up. Paul moved with a hunter's grace, slitting throats before cries of alarm could be raised. Bodies dropped into the soil, gurgling their final breaths. The final man turned to run, only to crash face-first into a wall of gnarled roots. Paul broke his neck with a twist and was at Mackenzie's side once more.

Violence was a necessary evil in the pursuit of justice, Paul rationalized. Engaging in these violent actions weighed heavily on Paul's conscience, but in the face of grave danger, there are times when one must make difficult choices to safeguard oneself and others.

His training in self-defense and combat came from his years in the military and, most recently, in the field as a police officer, honed through various cases and encounters over the course of his career as a detective. The skills were not learned in a traditional setting but rather forged in the crucible of real-world situations where split-second decisions can mean the difference between life and death. Paul abhors violence, but self-preservation sometimes means using violence.

Her clothing was thoroughly soaked with infection's poison. Mackenzie writhed as he cut away the ruined garb and cleaned the festering wound as best he could. All he had to offer was a prayer and what few herbs could be foraged in the darkness.

Dawn would find them again, but Mackenzie's state was grave. Only a miracle could carry her further.

Paul gathered her in his arms, determination like cold iron in his soul. He would reach sanctuary or perish in the attempt. Paul smeared mud across his skin, doing the same for Mackenzie with care, camouflage, and protection against the sun. Their flesh became one with the earthy hues of the rainforest floor.

Taking Mackenzie to a clinic or hospital would have exposed them to greater risks. The corruption ran deep, and they couldn't trust anyone outside their circle.

Paul's priority was to keep Mackenzie safe and hidden from those who sought to harm them. With limited options available, he had to rely on his own wits and resilience to navigate the treacherous waters of the island in our pursuit of justice.

Listening intently, Paul guided them among towering tree trunks, swirling fans of ferns, and curtains of hanging moss. Their scent and footfalls were disguised in the riotous chorus of the wilderness. Around them, enemies were closing.

Gunfire rang out steadily as patrols swept the terrain. One squad passed within arm's reach, yet the camouflaged fugitives remained unseen. They came upon a tiny clearing and froze. In the center, three men debated paths, uncaring that their quarry might be nearby. Paul held his breath, eyes locked with Mackenzie's. An eternity seemed to pass before the choice was made.

Onward they crept, stalking a nightmare of pursuit and deprivation. Dehydration pulled at Paul, but Mackenzie's fading strength demanded priority.

When refuge seemed beyond hope, a tiny stream traveled among the rocks. Its sweet waters revived their flagging bodies and minds.

As they knelt by the clear, trickling stream, their hands cupping the precious liquid, a sense of renewal washed over them. Mackenzie's voice, though weary, held a note of optimism as she whispered, "Water, the elixir of life. It's a small victory but one we sorely needed, Paul."

In response, Paul shared a nod of agreement, his own voice tinged with relief as he replied, "Indeed, Mackenzie. During all this darkness, even the smallest glimmer of light can guide us through.

This stream is a reminder that hope still flows during these troubling times."

The simple act of quenching their thirst from that stream served as a poignant reminder that amid the chaos and danger, there were still moments of reprieve and rejuvenation to be found. It was a brief interlude of peace during their tumultuous journey, a moment of unity and shared determination as they braced themselves for the trials that lay ahead.

Deeper into the lush labyrinth they fled, skirting discovery through earth, plants, and instincts alone. Their survival hung by the threads of stealth and luck. For now, it held true against the closing darkness. Mackenzie's heat-browned skin took on a ghastly pallor beneath its coating of mud and vegetation. Her breath shuddered weakly between cracked lips. Paul checked her pulse and suppressed a sob. It fluttered under his fingers like a dying bird's wings.

Each precious thready beat begged the question, how many more could she withstand?

He hoisted her limp form once more, her weight nothing to muscles gone past fatigue into some primal register beyond. Instinct and anger drove his limbs forward where conscious thought could no longer reach. Anger at those who'd brought them to this state. Anger because she deserved so much more than to perish alone in this green hell. He is angry because he refused to accept failure after coming so far.

Dawn's rose-gold light filtered through the canopy, outlining Paul as an avenging spirit emerged from the undergrowth. His eyes were pits of animalistic determination in mud-masked features. He would find sanctuary ahead or perish in the act of carrying her towards it. This he vowed silently as leaf and branch alike seemed to part for their passage. Survival remained a distant hope, but while life remained, there would be no surrender.

Paul eased Mackenzie's still form to the forest floor, camouflaging her beneath leaves and vines. His quest for sanctuary had become a race against time. Rifling through reserves of wilderness, he set about rigging snares along the game trails. Spears and stone-tipped projectiles were arranged where pursuing men would least expect.

Having garnered what intelligence he could from cracked patrol routines, Paul located the enemy's ad-hoc encampment. Well, after dark, he crawled its perimeter on elbows and knees, scouting for vulnerabilities.

At a carelessly masked storm culvert, he poured in a vial of homebrewed toxins. The resulting gaseous plumes would overwhelm in still air beneath the tents. His final snares were laid at the camp's exit points along with signs of disturbance, meant to draw the surviving hunters away at dawn.

Though outnumbered, the jungle would fight for him. Exhausted, Paul returned to Mackenzie's side as night gathered its cloak. Only restless dreams found him, of horrors lurking where lightlessness reigned. But come first light; this land would know justice or its denizen's death by his hand alone if need be.

Paul woke to a crash in the undergrowth and muffled oaths in an unfamiliar tongue. His traps had done their work. Snatching up his blade and a fallen prey's rifle, Paul launched himself at the nearest looming silhouette with a primal scream.

Steel bit deep before the man choked out his final breaths; gunfire roared across the foliage as more phantoms appeared, drawing Paul deeper into a nightmare frenzy. He was coiled with wrath and instinct now, an incarnation of the land's vengeance-given flesh. Blade and bullet wrought a grievous toll on his pursuers until only one remained, trembling and backing away with hands raised in plea. Paul's cracked lips peeled back, blood-flecked teeth glinting as he closed for the kill.

His visions shattered, leaving only merciless reality. Paul crumpled amid the carnage; all strength fled from limbs that refused to lift even as escape lay within sight. Through a gray haze, he saw silver waters sliding ceaselessly toward some far horizon. Salt kissed the air, bearing promises of hope or final respite.

Mackenzie.

He crawled on hands and knees, scraping flesh to bare sinew. Each inch gained was purchased with seeping wounds left behind in a crimson snail's trail. Her pallid form came into view, her face upturned to a mercifully overcast sky.

Paul gathered her in shaking arms. Gritting his teeth, he began shuffling forward toward the water. Sand shifted treacherously under raw palms as salty spray stung open gashes. The whole of his existence narrowed to placing one foot in front of the other. Delirium and excruciating agony vied for dominance as muscles spasmed in protest. Still, he pulled himself and her body ever onward, driven by love and sheer cussed will alone.

As the tideline came into view, a dark shape merged from the roiling seas. Salvation had arrived, or a cruel joke of fickle fate. Paul's grasp on reality finally came, and they collapsed into the breakers as aid reached down to drag them from the brink.

Strong hands lifted Paul and Mackenzie from the surf, laying them on weathered wood. Familiar faces swam in Paul's fading vision, mouths forming urgent words he could no longer grasp. Through the gathering haze came snatches of voices long thought lost to these harsh shores. A cool draught was tipped between parched lips as splinters jabbed his ruined flesh.

Then, firm hands eased him into the cool darkness, carrying his ravaged body away from this place of twisted dreams and memories. Fever set in as the sea tossed them toward unknown fates, Paul clinging to the last fraying threads of Mackenzie's life alongside his own. Would sanctuary finally be found? Or had they traveled so far only to meet some crueler end beyond these waves' breaking? Past evils still lurked amid St. Anne's shadows, clinging to power by twisted roots sunk deep.

Time alone would reveal their destiny. For now, all that remained was to surrender to the embrace of the deep and pray the tomorrow's light would break kind upon their faces. This, the final hope before darkness took them both at last into its eternal caress.

CHAPTER FOURTEEN

One Last Stand

THE UNEXPECTED TURN OF EVENTS BROUGHT PAUL AND MACKENZIE salvation in the form of allies they never imagined they had. They whisked Paul and Mackenzie away to a secure location far from the prying eyes of their enemies, providing them with much-needed medical care and a respite from the relentless pursuit.

They were taken to a secluded, safe house nestled in the heart of the forest. The place exuded an air of secrecy, shielded from prying eyes by thick foliage and cleverly camouflaged entrances. Inside, the walls whispered tales of past inhabitants, each scar telling a story of survival and defiance against looming threats. It was a haven amid chaos, a place where trust and solidarity thrived in the face of adversity.

The rescuers were a group of dedicated locals who had been silently watching the escalating turmoil on the island. They were not affiliated with the police, fishermen, politicians, or journalists but rather ordinary citizens who had enough of the corruption plaguing their community. Their courage and sense of justice aligned with Paul's and Mackenzie's, leading them to intervene in their time of need and offering them a chance to regroup and continue the fight against the darkness that threatened St. Anne.

Mackenzie and Paul were patched up and given time to recuperate, which enabled them to gather their strength for the challenges that lay ahead. After a few days of recovery and strategic planning, they ventured back into the jungle, renewed in purpose and resolve to finish what they started in their quest for truth and justice on St.

Anne.

After regaining their strength and resolve, Mackenzie and Paul set up a makeshift camp deep in the heart of the jungle, where the dense foliage provided cover and protection. Their mission was clear: it was time for one final stand against the forces of corruption that had plagued St. Anne for far too long. Armed with the truth and a renewed sense of purpose, they prepared to confront their enemies head-on and see justice served once and for all.

Paul scanned the dense jungle behind them, watching for any signs of pursuit through the fading light. He turned to Mackenzie, her face looking much better since her medical care and rest. "We'll make our stand here," he said.

They worked quickly to prepare, clearing brush and twisting vines into makeshift bindings. Paul assembled their meager supplies of bullets and blades while Mackenzie surveyed the terrain for any tactical advantages. As night fell, they hunkered down to wait, exhaustion battling adrenaline.

Not long after night fall, as they huddled by the crackling fire, a sense of foreboding settled over them, the rustling of leaves in the distance signaling the approach of their pursuers.

In hushed tones, Paul's words carried a weight of urgency and determination. "Mackenzie," he began, his voice low yet resolute, "They're closing in. We must be prepared for whatever comes our way."

Her gaze met his, rigid determination reflecting in her eyes as she replied, "We've faced worse odds, Paul. We'll stand our ground and fight if we must."

The tension hung thick in the air, each passing moment bringing them closer to the inevitable confrontation. As the sound of footsteps grew louder, a sense of grim resolve settled over them, their hearts beating in sync with the pulse of the jungle.

The crackle of undergrowth announced the enemy's approach.

Paul peeked through parted branches to observe their stalkers silhouetted against the gloom, six armed figures sweeping methodically through the trees. He tapped Mackenzie and pointed, readying their ambush. When the squad emerged, Paul and Mackenzie launched their attack.

A hail of gunfire and flying traps scattered the men. In the chaos, Paul scrambled from cover, slashing at legs and slamming his rifle butt into heads. Mackenzie wielded a machete with lethal ferocity, hacking a path to reclaim their guns.

Paul battled on, fighting through pain and exhaustion as the squad gained ground. He and Mackenzie stood back-to-back, fending off vicious blows. But the enemies pressed ever closer, unyielding as the tide.

When Paul's gun clicked empty, he braced for the final stand. But then a shot rang out from the trees, and an enemy fell. More shots followed, picking off the squad one by one as figures emerged from the jungle's edge.

Through the clash of steel and shots echoing into the night, a familiar voice called Paul's name. He turned to see reinforcements had arrived, former comrades who now stood against corruption to aid those fighting for justice. With renewed allies, the tide swiftly turned against the squad.

In the heat of the moment, as allies rallied to their side, faces were familiar, but many names faded into insignificance compared to the united front that was presented against their foes. What mattered most was the shared resolve to combat corruption and ensure justice prevailed on the island. The bond forged in that crucial moment transcended individual identities, strengthening their collective determination to see the fight through to the end.

When the battle finally ceased, Paul surveyed the fallen enemies as waves lapped the stained shore. Victory had been achieved but at great cost. He took Mackenzie's hand, sheathing his blade to embark on the next chapter's unwinding mysteries and chances for redemption.

Mackenzie and Paul blinked in disbelief as Officers Clarke and Silva rushed onto the sand, firing precision shots in the moonlit gloom. They engaged the remaining squad members with practiced coordination, disarming and subduing them with efficient strikes.

As the last enemy crumpled, Clarke laughed and pulled Paul into a weary hug. "You didn't think we'd miss the fun, did you?" Silva clapped his back, grinning through the dirt and blood. They had gone deep undercover in the department to expose corruption from within.

Mackenzie sobbed with relief, embracing her partners gratefully. Though outnumbered and outgunned, their combined forces had prevailed against the squad. Justice had allies in even the most unexpected places, ready to stand up for what was right when it mattered most.

When officers Clark and Silva came to their aid in this dark hour, the exchange of words was of relief, gratitude, and a shared sense of camaraderie in the face of imminent danger. As they emerged from the shadows, their presence was a welcome sight in the chaos that surrounded them.

Mackenzie and Paul exchanged a glance that spoke volumes, a silent acknowledgment of the risks we had all faced and the unspoken bond that united us at that moment. Officer Clark's voice broke through the tense silence, his tone firm yet comforting as he said, "We've got your backs, Phillips. Let's finish this together."

Paul could see the glint of determination in Silva's eyes as he nodded in agreement, his silent support a testament to the solidarity they had forged in the crucible of their shared ordeal.

Mackenzie's voice resonated with gratitude as she replied, "Thank you. We couldn't have made it this far without your help. Let's show them what we're made of."

And with those words of solidarity and unity, they all stood together, a formidable force against the darkness that threatened to engulf us. In that fleeting moment of connection and shared purpose, they found strength in each other's presence, ready to face the final showdown that awaited with courage and unwavering determination.

With their enemies defeated and the friends reunited, Paul smiled through his pain, knowing their long fight was closer to the truth and redemption they sought. He sagged against a fallen palm, the soil gritty against his torn skin. Exhaustion pulled at his frayed senses.

But as Clarke and Silva engaged the remaining hunters, he saw an enemy break free, sprinting for the tree line with a stolen blade in his hand. Rage and duty flooded Paul's limbs with fresh adrenaline. He lurched from his shelter and gave chase. The hunter dodged Silva's shots, cutting into shadow and vine. But Paul was relentless, tracking each snapped twig and footfall in the brush. When the man scrambled onto an outcropping, Paul sprang.

They grappled, weapons forgotten, an exchange of raw brutality fueled by desperation. Paul slammed his foe onto the ragged rock, punching until bone and cliff met in ruin. Breathlessly, he rolled to his back, staring at the moon through a filter of leaves. By the time Paul returned to camp, the battle was done.

Clarke bound the last surviving hunter while Silva tended to wounds by flashlight. Their foes were vanquished, but the fight was far from over. With reinforcements by their side and fire in their eyes, Paul and his allies would press on towards justice's dawn.

But first, much needed sleep. Each person would take an hour of guard duty to ensure their safety, while the others refreshed themselves with much needed rest. Paul was the first to succumb to exhaustion.

He awoke to the clean scent of pine and antiseptic smoke. Soft voices filled the glow of a saline lamp as deft hands cleaned and sealed his wounds. Mackenzie sat at his side, exhaustion clinging to her brows like dew.

She smiled as his eyes met hers. "Clarke and Silva stabilized you," she whispered.

The mayor's henchmen didn't survive their crimes. Justice was served, for now.

Unbeknownst to Paul, Clarke and Silva had called for backup. Backup they trusted. He only realized when the sounds of police and ambulance sirens rose with the dawn.

As the additional officers and medical help arrived, they carted away the arrested and fallen. The goon squad's mission had been retaliation for their comrades' defeat, a threat meant to stamp out resistance. But Paul's and Mackenzie's determination, along with their allies, only strengthened their willingness to stand against corruption wherever it hid.

Clarke emerged as Silva packed their truck.

"The mayor and his regime have been detained," Clarke reported, grinning. Their network exposed by evidence Paul and Mackenzie risked everything to obtain.

"Rest," he told them. Recovery awaited, as was rebuilding on stable ground.

Bringing news of the mayor's arrest, a wave of relief washed over Paul and Mackenzie, signaling a momentary respite from the chaos that had consumed their existence. A sense of closure beckoned, offering Paul and Mackenzie a chance to heal from the wounds, both physical and emotional, that had accumulated along their perilous path.

Guided by Clark and Silva, they journeyed to a secluded mountain retreat, a sanctuary shrouded in tranquility. The crisp mountain air carried whispers of restoration, promising comfort to their weary souls.

The Havenwood Retreat was nestled atop the mist-shrouded peaks of the Emerald Ridge Mountains. It conveyed an aura of ancient wisdom and tranquility, its sprawling grounds enveloped in a canopy of whispering pines and emerald ferns.

A winding path led them through a verdant forest, the earthy scent of moss and pine needles infusing the air with a sense of serenity. As they approached the main lodge, the grandeur of Havenwood revealed itself in all its splendor. Crafted from weathered timber and adorned with intricate carvings, the lodge stood as a testament to a bygone era where nature and man coexisted in harmony.

Inside, the interior was a symphony of warmth and light, the crackling hearth casting a soft glow over handwoven tapestries and plush furnishings. Sunlight filtered through stained glass windows, casting kaleidoscopic patterns on polished wooden floors.

Mackenzie's eyes widened in awe at the sight, her gaze taking in the intricate details of the sanctuary.

"Paul," she murmured, a sense of wonder threading through her voice, "This place is fantastic. I have never been here before. Have you?"

"No, I have never been here, but I have heard others talk about it."

Havenwood offered Paul and Mackenzie a sanctuary from the storms that raged beyond its tranquil borders. It was a place of healing, comfort, and reflection, a place where the whispers of the mountains and the rustling of the trees carried tales of hope and renewal.

Privacy away from public eyes was just what they needed to heal.

As they settled in, the gentle support of a local doctor and his nurse tended to their wounds, their hands softly healing with each gentle touch. The scent of healing herbs mingled with the crackling of a soothing fire, creating a tapestry of comfort and rejuvenation.

Mackenzie, ever the resilient spirit, finally allowed herself to exhale, her features softening in a rare moment of vulnerability.

"Paul," she spoke softly, her voice a mere whisper in the peaceful ambiance, "We've made it through the storm. It's time to rest and let the healing begin."

And so, under the watchful gaze of the mountains, they surrendered to much-needed rest, allowing the healing hands of time and care to mend the scars that marred their bodies and souls. It was a moment of reprieve in this tumultuous time in their lives, a moment to heal and prepare for the challenges that awaited them beyond the sanctuary of the mountain retreat.

The following week, after leaving the comfort of Havenwood, fully recuperated and rested, Paul and Mackenzie were welcomed by the masses when they reached the courthouse.

Inside, islanders packed pews behind prosecutors presenting their case. Paul's testimony sealed the corrupt regime's fate, their crimes laid bare by his tenacious pursuit of truth.

His eye caught Kim Wong in the gallery, digitally chronicling justice's arduous process. Her stories helped spark solidarity that toppled oppression and bloomed renewal.

The trial that unfolded in the wake of the mayor's arrest lasted for a span of three tumultuous weeks. Three weeks filled with gripping testimonies, impassioned arguments, and the relentless pursuit of truth in a courtroom pulsating with the weight of justice. Each day brought new revelations, new challenges to overcome, and new obstacles to confront as the wheels of justice turned with unwavering determination. Witnesses were called, the evidence presented, and the scales of justice balanced on a razor's edge as the fate of the mayor hung in the balance.

Throughout those intense weeks, Paul and Mackenzie stood as steadfast sentinels of truth, their resolve unwavering in the face of adversity.

The trial became a crucible of fire, testing the spirit of all involved as the echoes of past transgressions reverberated through the hallowed halls of the courthouse.

And when the final gavel struck, signaling the end of the trial, a sense of closure descended upon them, a solemn reminder of the power of justice served and the enduring legacy of those who stand firm in the pursuit of truth.

Three weeks of trial, three weeks of relentless pursuit of justice, a testament to the enduring spirit of those who fight for what is right, no matter the cost.

In the defendants' box, hatred met righteousness as the gavel fell, the verdict of guilty ringing out for all to hear. As the final verdict was read in the courthouse, a mix of emotions washed over Paul. Relief, vindication, and a sense of closure filled his heart.

All the struggles, the risks, and the sacrifices made in the pursuit of truth and justice culminated in that moment of accountability for the guilty parties. As their deeds were laid bare and justice was served, a profound sense of satisfaction washed over him, knowing that their efforts had not been in vain. It was a moment of triumph, not just for Paul, but for all those who believed in fighting for what was right and just.

After the trial had ended, Paul stood on the courthouse steps, Mackenzie at his side, surveying a community that was embracing the victory. Though darkness still clung to some hearts, the people had reclaimed their power through unity against the tyrants who held them captive.

Bright purpose filled Paul once more as he bid farewell to friends, new and old. The island was in capable hands, healing and accountable. His mission was fulfilled, and the innocent was avenged. Now, their stories could inspire others to stand up for justice wherever shadows lurked, guiding more to freedom through solidarity and light.

Further indictments and arrests followed as swiftly as tides. Familiar faces paraded past the press in zip cuffs became points on career-ending flowcharts revealing a cancer society once denied. The tyranny that once strangled villages vanished under democratic sunlight, hope sprouting where fear once thrived.

That afternoon, Mackenzie met Paul at the shore in front of his bungalow, where the surf greeted their weary feet. The gentle lull of the waves provided a soothing backdrop to their conversation; a conversation tinged with the weight of past battles and the hope for a brighter future.

Mackenzie's gaze met Paul's, her eyes reflecting the turbulent emotions swirling within her. "Paul," she began, her voice a whisper carried by the salty breeze, "It's finally over. Justice has been served, but at what cost?"

He turned to her, his expression a mirror of empathy and understanding. "Every battle leaves scars, Mackenzie," he replied, his voice a calming presence. "But with each scar comes a reminder of our resilience and our unyielding commitment to what is right."

She nodded, a flicker of determination igniting in her eyes. "We've been through so much, Paul, but we've emerged stronger because of it."

As the sun dipped below the horizon, casting a golden glow over the turbulent seas, they stood side by side, united in their shared journey of trials and triumphs, a testament to the enduring bond forged through fire and steel.

A few days later, at the market square, families Paul fought beside unveiled monuments to honor guardians who lit their darkest nights. He traced Jane's name etched smoothly and proudly. He wondered if she would ever return to what the island had offered as their thanks to her. A child pressed a hand-stitched flower, hope personified, and Paul's heart swelled sure that goodness grew where tyranny once thrived.

On the town's streets, dancing and music rose in melodies. Liberation rang from every joyous shout, escaping lips oppressed too long. Paul saw in each face beaming the power of unity that toppled evil clinging to control and drowned out lies with love and truth.

Though battles remained, to this day, he savored victory in the community as they embraced its sovereignty. With Mackenzie at his side, gratitude and hope for budding democracy sustained him on the journeys ahead. Here was redemption enough, born of just.

He said his farewells along the shore as waves brushed reflections of a brighter dawn. Clarke and Silva clasped his shoulder with pride for the progress that was made, Kim with hopes their stories would spread justice's seed. Mackenzie embraced him longest, etching each feature to memory as new paths diverged into unknown.

As they stood by the skiff, ready to embark on the final leg of his journey, the weight of their shared experiences bore heavily upon them. The air crackled with tension, yet beneath it lay a silent understanding between them, a bond forged in the fires of adversity.

Mackenzie's eyes shone resolve and lingering exhaustion as she turned to Paul, her voice steady but tinged with a hint of vulnerability, "Paul, we've come a long way. Whatever happens next, I want you to know that I'm grateful for your guidance and your unwavering determination."

Paul met her gaze with a nod of respect, acknowledging the trials they had faced and the obstacles that had been overcome. His voice, edged with a rare note of sincerity, replied, "Mackenzie, your strength and dedication speak to your character. We may face great peril ahead but know that I trust you to watch my back as I watch yours. Let's see this through to the end, side by side."

The sun was setting over the horizon, casting a golden hue over the water as Paul prepared to depart St. Anne. Mackenzie could not hide the concern etched on her face.

"Mackenzie," his tone steady yet with a hint of farewell in it. "Leaving St. Anne wasn't a choice I made lightly. There are shadows creeping in, I need time away to refocus."

She eyed Paul with a mix of understanding and worry. "Paul, you can't chase every specter of the past. St. Anne needs you; we need you."

He gave her a rare smile, touched by her concern. "I know, Mackenzie. But sometimes, the shadows of yesterday grow too long to ignore. Trust me, I'll return when the time is right."

And with that, he boarded the skiff, the gentle lapping of the water serving as a bittersweet farewell to a place that held both solace and unanswered questions.

In that moment of shared understanding and unspoken camaraderie, Paul boarded the skiff, ready to confront whatever fate had in store for him. The words they had exchanged lingered in the air, a silent promise of mutual support and resilience as he braced himself for what the future would bring.

He settled in the skiff, surveying a community reforging itself free from shadows that no longer existed. Purpose guided him elsewhere to what he hoped would be an uneventful return to retirement. His legacy here was but a ripple, though tides of change continued swelling.

On distant shores, new injustices would be waiting to be exposed; different souls may be yearning for the courage he inspired to combat darkness, but for now, he wanted no part. Though risks remained in his life, he knew redemption's flame could not be quenched that lit within him to serve wherever he needed most. He needed a break. He would return one day. Soon? Later? He had no idea. He considered St. Anne his home, but he needed a break.

As St. Anne began to disappear from view, faces that lifted him stayed etched in Paul's heart, their bright smiles telling him the battle was never one man's alone. He was but one person, and where it led him next, more righteousness would bloom for freedom's eternal harvest.

The fishing boat crossed the horizon, and St. Anne dissolved into the vast, unknowable blue stretching ahead. Paul gazed into its shimmering promise and let the past's waves fade from his shoulders' crests.

Chapter Fifteen

Paradise Regained

THE GENTLE BREEZE CARRIED THE SCENT OF FRANGIPANI THROUGH the open windows of Paul's seaside hut. Three months had passed since he last saw the shores of St. Anne fading in the distance, and in that time, his wounds had fully mended. Each morning, he would emerge from his hut to find the island awakening around him, the call of birds mingling with the laughter of children playing in the surf.

Paul had found refuge in this nameless key, its isolation, offering the relief he needed to recover from the trials of his last stand. As he strode along the powdery beach, circling the outline of his wounds with his fingers, he marveled at how quickly the flesh had knitted together.

But some scars went deeper than skin, the memories of battle and corruption still lingered in his dreams. Slowly, however, even those memories were beginning to fade, replaced by more peaceful images of the simple life this island afforded.

For the first time in a long while, Paul felt at peace, his mind and body fully healed. He greeted the sunrise each day with something closer to hope than he had known in ages.

As the days blended into weeks, Paul found himself gravitating more fully into the rhythms of island life. When not dwelling on memories of the past, he offered aid wherever it was needed, mending fishing nets on the docks and helping to thatch new roofs as the rainy season set in.

The villagers quickly came to see him as one of their own,

drawn to his quiet strength and work ethic. Word soon spread of Paul's history with the corrupt regime on St. Anne, and the people begged for his counsel. They had lived so long under tyranny that the mere idea of true democracy was foreign. But Paul patiently guided them, advising town halls and working with newly elected officials to establish fair process and accountability.

Gradually, with Paul's assistance, transparency and trust began to take root where fear and secrecy had thrived for decades. The islanders' faith in their leadership and justice system was restored, a reminder that light often emerges from darkness if only one keeps striving with patience, wisdom, and care for humanity.

As Paul witnessed the transformation, he found purpose in helping this community rebuild from the ashes of its past. His efforts would ensure that a new dawn had risen and a bright future was within their reach.

As the months slipped by, Paul was surprised to receive a visitor; Mackenzie had tracked him down, bearing gifts of dried fish and fruits from their home islands. They shared stories late into the night, bonding further over bottles of local rum. She spoke of the progress being made to reform the police on St. Anne but confessed they sorely needed guidance.

 Mackenzie's sudden arrival was like a beacon of hope in the storm. Her determination and unwavering support convinced Paul that returning to St. Anne was the right path. She painted a picture of a community in need of justice and restoration, compelling Paul to join the fight once more.

Paul agreed to return with her, eager to continue their mission.

Upon returning to St. Anne, Paul decided to start fresh and chose a new place to call home. The memories of the past were too intertwined with his old bungalow, so a new beginning felt necessary.

Paul's new home is a quaint cottage nestled among lush tropical foliage with pleasant views. The interior is cozy and welcoming, with comfortable furnishings and warm, earthy tones. From the windows, Paul can see towering palm trees swaying gently in the tropical breeze and catch glimpses of the azure ocean beyond.

It's slightly smaller than Paul's previous bungalow, but the space feels more intimate and suited to his current needs. It's a peaceful sanctuary where he can continue to reflect on the past and embrace the future with hope.

He worked closely with Mackenzie, now a lieutenant, to completely overhaul police training procedures and establish a new code of conduct. Using his vast experience, Paul schooled young recruits in detection skills, forensic practices, and upholding civil rights.

Most importantly, he instilled in them a fierce commitment to justice and protecting the vulnerable. For the first time, the people of St. Anne knew they had advocates in their local police force, not oppressors. Paul took great pride in seeing his students excelling and gaining the trust of their communities.

His work with Mackenzie became the most fulfilling part of Paul's days. Even as a consultant, Paul still fought injustice side by side with Mackenzie, but now with optimism, having equipped new generations to continue the relay. Their bond only deepened, finding purpose and camaraderie in rebuilding the island from the group up.

As the seasons blended into one another, Paul came to realize how tightly woven he had become into the fabric of this tiny community. Where he had originally seen only a place of temporary refuge, he now regarded the island as home, its familiar landmarks, flavors, and routines providing the steady rhythm his journey-weary soul craved.

Each vibrant sunset igniting the darkening sea only deepened his affection for these shores. The local fishermen had become his brothers, regaling him with tales over glasses of rum punch as waves lapped at the docks. The laughter of children racing the tide never failed to lift his spirit.

Even nature displayed her beauty in a new light to Paul now.

Every sunrise seemed to outdo the last in vibrant hues; every wave crashing against the reef carried Nature's majestic song. For the first time in memory, he felt truly anchored, not constrained, but buoyed by roots of his own choosing.

This place had healed wounds far deeper than flesh. Its people had breathed life into his soul once more. As Paul gazed out over cobalt seas, he was struck by an epiphany: after decades adrift, he had found belonging at the end of the earth. This remote paradise had become the home his battered heart always desired.

Yet, for all the contentment Paul had found, the sea in his soul would not fully rest. Word reached the shores that, on a neighboring island, tyranny was thriving where transparency should have been rooted. Reports told of "accidental" deaths in custody, rigged elections, and exploitation of the poor continuing unchecked. It was in Paul's nature to chafe at such injustice, especially where he saw parallels with his past battles on St. Anne.

One evening, as storms rolled in, a bedraggled messenger arrived seeking him. They came from an island in the outer chain and were begging for his counsel. Tales of corruption there stirred the restlessness in Paul's heart once more.

He knew that turning a blind eye would go against all he had come to stand for. As he packed provisions that night by lamplight, a part of him yearned to remain lost in the rhythms of this quiet life. But a greater force was at play, one that had shaped his destiny since youth, the call to stand with the oppressed wherever dark forces conspired. With reluctance and resolve in equal measure, Paul readied to embark at dawn, lighting once more into the fray.

That night, as the wind whipped the treetops into a frenzy, Paul paced his home, torn by indecision. Part of him yearned to accept the call and immerse himself once more in purpose, to deploy his keen detective skills and experience fighting corruption wherever it reared its head. But the life he had built here offered solace like nothing else. After so many years battling injustice, perhaps he deserved the simple pleasures of retirement in this secluded paradise. His mind wandered to memories of evenings spent laughing with friends on the docks as sunset painted the clouds.

Mackenzie understood his struggle, as always.

"Some battles are worth fighting, but right here is where you're needed most now," she reminded him gently. Paul knew she spoke wisdom; his skills could help many, yet abandoning the only real home he had ever known would leave an ache in his soul.

As streaks of lightning cracked the sky, Paul gazed out over thrashing treetops, lost in thought. This community had given him belonging after so much instability. Could he, in good conscience, turn his back now to chase battles elsewhere? His destiny had never been clear cut; perhaps his true duty lay in defending what he had come to cherish most. The storm raged into the night, mirroring Paul's turmoil as he weighed loyalty to purpose against that to home and family.

As dawn light filtered through waving palms, Paul's decision was made. He met Mackenzie on the beach to say farewell, the bittersweetness of departure weighing heavy in their hearts.

"You brought light to the shadows of my past," Paul told her. "Never doubt that the lives we've saved make all of it worth it."

They embraced, holding tight to fleeting moments as waves rushed the shore. Paul made his rounds, offering gratitude to the fisherfolk who had become brothers and sisters to his soul. Each hug and clasp of hands was etched into his memory, kindling flickers of sorrow amid resolve.

Paul was glad to have found purpose here defending his chosen family, yet could not deny the solace of their acceptance and care in his twilight years. He had come to this place a broken man and was left whole, all because of their shared struggles and laughter along life's journey.

That evening, Paul penned a letter to Mackenzie by lamplight, pouring his heart onto the page. He spoke of how their battles against corruption had reawakened purpose in his retirement. Fighting oppression side by side rekindled his long-dormant spirit of service. Though conflict called him elsewhere now, this little community would forever stand as a beacon of light in his wanderings. Their shared struggles battling tyranny bound their spirits together across any distance.

Paul promised that though the sea would once more separate them, these shores and the bonds of justice linking all who defended truth would remain etched in his soul till the end of his days. He also promised to return. Someday.

At dawn, Paul handed Mackenzie the letter with an embrace, braving final farewells before boarding the prop plane. As islands fell away below, Paul peered through misty windows, committing vibrant landscapes and dear faces to memory's keeping. His years here affirmed that light and hope arise wherever compassion for humanity prevails against darkness.

Though duty beckoned Paul to new adversaries, these tranquil shores would forever signify redemption of a place, a purpose, and a weary soul reawakened by the resilient spirit of a people who refused to lose faith in tomorrow's promise of justice. His story found its fitting end, and a future blazed ahead as bright as these people's unwavering hope.

Paul gazed out the plane's circular window as waves of cloud obscured any last glimpses of the speck that had become his longed-for haven. Yet even through wisps of vapor, rays of sunrise sprayed the sky with hope, a reminder that light prevails where darkness holds temporary sway. His thoughts lingered on those who had breathed renewed purpose into his twilight years.

Fighting injustice by their sides rekindled fires long thought extinguished, reforging his spirit into the champion of justice his destiny demanded. Though new missions were called, his heart would forever carry the torch lit by that steadfast community.

As the plane cut swiftly across boundless azure, Paul felt untethered yet anchored, unmoored by duty's summons yet bolstered by roots too deep for any tempest to unearth. Wherever oppression reared its vile head, he would be there to defend the oppressed. For his gift and curse was defending hope wherever it flickered against tyranny's grim grip.

And so, Paul's saga fittingly ends as it began, poised on the cusp of unknown horizons, guided by light kindled within his soul and fueled by the resilience of spirits who taught that defiance itself is beauty's purest form. His was an eternal battle for justice, but walking its path alongside rays of such radiance redeemed even its costliest trials. Dawn ushered in a new day, and he was to meet it, as it had always been and would ever be, ablaze with purpose.

Paul began looking forward to returning to St. Anne.

About the Author

Dr. Philip DeLizio, Ed. D., is a former classroom teacher. Upon his retirement, his focus became writing: inspirational books for teens and young adults based on his experiences teaching, hoping his words would be inspirational and uplifting to his readers. He also writes adult mysteries based in the Caribbean.

Dr. DeLizio' has several degrees, including a Doctorate Degree in Education. He loves traveling and enjoying his morning coffee.

www.ingramcontent.com/pod-product-compliance
Lightning Source LLC
Chambersburg PA
CBHW040145160726
48006CB00014B/1623